DAUGHTER

DAUGHTER

Claudia Dey

FARRAR, STRAUS AND GIROUX

NEW YORK

Farrar, Straus and Giroux
120 Broadway, New York 10271

The following sources were quoted and paraphrased: Marguerite Duras,
The Pretenders, Giancarlo DiTrapano, Godless, William Shakespeare,
Annie Hamilton, Joan Acocella, Rachel Cusk, Sam Mendes, Virginia Woolf,
and Joy Division. Grateful acknowledgement is made for permission
to use the headline quoted from the pages of *People* on page 63. © 1988
Meredith Operations Corporation. All rights reserved. Reprinted from
People and published with permission of Meredith Operations Corporation.
Reproduction in any manner in any language in whole or in part without
written permission is prohibited.

Library of Congress Cataloging-in-Publication Data
Names: Dey, Claudia, author.
Title: Daughter / Claudia Dey.
Description: First American edition. | New York : Farrar, Straus and
Giroux, 2023. |
Identifiers: LCCN 2023013724 | ISBN 9780374609702 (hardback)
Subjects: LCGFT: Novels.
Classification: LCC PR9199.3.D492 D38 2023 | DDC 813/.54—
dc23/eng/20230330
LC record available at https://lccn.loc.gov/2023013724

Designed by Kate Sinclair

www.fsgbooks.com
www.twitter.com/fsgbooks • www.facebook.com/fsgbooks

1   3   5   7   9   10   8   6   4   2

The author acknowledges the financial support of the
Canada Council for the Arts.

DAUGHTER

ONE

The only time I get to be close to my father is when he is betraying his life.

When my father is not betraying his life, I hardly hear from him.

So, whenever my father, Paul, texts to say that he needs me, and can we get together, it's urgent, my husband will caution, Are you sure that's a good idea?

And leaving the apartment, I answer, But he is my father.

.   .   .

At night, I try to make sense of what I have lost.

I dream about my younger sister, Eva.

After Paul's affair with Lee, Eva estranged herself from me. Eva is my father's only daughter with my stepmother, Cherry. Eva's letter announcing her estrangement arrived in the mail shortly before my first play opened. I was on my way to the theatre for the final dress rehearsal when her letter came. The envelope was thin, the return address Eva's liberal arts college, where she was in her freshman year, studying philosophy. I read the letter standing in the foyer of my apartment building. Above me, black wires hung loose from the ceiling like entrails. The exposed wires had been there when I moved into the building. Then, they alarmed me. Now, they were fact. Eva's letter was tightly handwritten in blue ink, three-quarters of a page long. Eva was cutting off contact. She told me she kept only good and trustworthy people in her life. My recent behaviour as Paul's confidante throughout his affair with Lee demonstrated I was neither good nor trustworthy. Eva broke down what it was to be good and what it was to be trustworthy, as it was clear I had no grasp of their meaning. Being good and trustworthy were conditions to remain in Eva's life. I did not meet the conditions to remain in Eva's life. As a result of failing to meet these conditions, I was no longer Eva's sister. Her decision was irreversible. She had no interest in hearing my side of the story. Don't bother trying to present it to me, she wrote. Eva was relieved to be free of my self-dramatizing. She was sure I'd turn her pain into a play, and call it art. This only underscored my nature which was lazy and deceitful. Our father said she had a dangerous remove when I was the one with the dangerous remove. I was sick and sly and I had stolen her every happiness. She had thought of us as bonded for life. She had taken to heart the way I rejected the term "half-sister." *I refuse to make a fraction out of a relationship I feel is more than whole.* Your words, not mine, Eva wrote. Well, she wrote, like everything you do, your love has been a performance. You do not hold yourself to any sort of standard.

Because of that, you will always be lost and reckless. She felt sorry for anyone who got close to me. I would only destroy them. Don't ever try to defend yourself to me, Eva wrote. My mind is made up. You are no longer my sister—she restated the purpose of her letter, and at its end, signed her name in the same careful hand. *Evangeline*.

I do not know who was the parasite, who was the host. By then Paul and I were indistinguishable, locked by mutual need. The night he confessed his affair with Lee to Cherry was the night everything came apart for my father and me. Earlier that day, I met Paul for coffee. He told me of his plan to confess to Cherry that night. Paul had a dejected look to him, he said he felt beaten down by his situation. I reached for Paul's hand, but he flinched and withheld it. He read my expression, and told me with some annoyance not to feel sorry for him, his situation was of his own doing. Paul did not know what outcome he wanted in confessing to Cherry, only that he could not go on lying. He had hit his breaking point. He had been with Cherry for eighteen years. What kind of man was he? He was a coward. He could not live this double life. He did not know himself anymore. He did not know his own heart. He was a writer for God's sake, and he no longer had a view into himself. It was the loneliest feeling. Maybe he would never write again. His eyes skipped over me like I was a pretty stranger. He was risking everything and for what. Was he in love with Lee? Who knows. Was he in love with Cherry? It did not seem likely given the fact that he had cheated on her, not just cheated, but felt deeply for another woman for over two years. But was it love? How could he not know? Maybe he was incapable of love? Paul asked this last question in an exasperated tone, he had built to this last question, and I felt the way I did when I listened to Paul read from his novel *Daughter*, that listening to my father was like listening to a piece of music. Then his brow furrowed, his focus narrowed and he drove his eyes deep into mine. If he left Cherry, Paul said, Eva would never speak to him again. There is this to consider, Paul said. There's Eva.

As Paul was confessing to Cherry, I was on the other side of the city in my apartment. I looked around the rooms and did not know where to place my body. I lay on the floor of the living room, and then sat on the ancient kitchen counter. I kept my phone in my dress pocket, I waited for Paul to call me from a hotel or text from his study, for Paul to call me from a stoplight near our place, what's the address again, he was on his way. Paul could take our bed. Wes could sleep on the couch. I would be fine on the floor. I kept checking my phone, nothing changed. I found a pack of cigarettes in the freezer, I raised our front window, leaned out and smoked. Below me, a boy rode by on his bicycle. He was momentarily blindfolded by his hair, his friends rode past him. The ciga-rette was stale, I had been trying to quit. I stubbed out the cigarette and flushed it down the toilet. I sometimes got takeout from the bar around the corner, and when the chef saw me smoking, he told me I was too beautiful to smoke, if I smoked, I would wreck my face. Now I stood before the bathroom mirror, trying to see what the chef had seen. The chef felt I needed protection. Throughout Paul's affair with Lee, my father and I spoke constantly. We talked on the phone at odd hours, met for dinner every chance we could. Paul wanted my view on love. When he listened, he was not just attentive but acquisitive. He used my feelings to clarify his own, internalizing them so totally, he believed he was their author. Paul took for himself all that I saw and felt. I gave freely because I could. I conjured new insight, my insight multiplied. I could not be diminished. I was the light source upon which Paul drew, the inverse was just as true, and like that, we fed each other. For Lee, we shopped for gold. I delivered gifts to her apartment building. With every secret act, we increased our closeness until we fused. I could not stand the prospect of slipping back into that angry grey world of before with no hidden current of electricity between us. When Paul was with Lee, I was loved by my father. Without Paul's love, I was powerless. I had no gravitational pull.

It was evening when Paul and Cherry sat down together in their kitchen. The sun was low and distant, but still shone faintly in the room, as if trying to get a hold of it. There was something desperate about the sun. The kitchen was a modern space, glassed in. It overlooked a large backyard which gave way to the ravine that ran through the west end of the city. The boundary between Paul and Cherry's yard and the ravine was fenced off. Vines covered the fence, lacing together like fingers. At the centre of the fence was a gate with a combination lock. The gate opened onto a rugged stone path that led steeply down to a pond. To Cherry's eye, the pond was green and polluted. The pond would sulk for months then grow vengeful. It would rise against its shore-line, and when it did, Cherry blamed the pond for chilling the house. She pulled on a sweater, turned her face to the glass. Outside it was spring, and her garden was in bloom. Cherry called the daffodils flamboyant. Despite the tension he felt, Paul laughed and agreed. Cherry had a way with words. He and Cherry had a comfortable life made possible by beautiful objects. Upstairs, Eva was in her bedroom, at her desk, studying diligently for her final exams. She was in her last month of high school. She had already been accepted to a prestigious private women's college for the following year, but was determined to get the highest grades in her class. Earlier, Eva had masked her face in white cold cream. She had put the jar of cold cream in the freezer, and then she had coated her delicate face in the freezing cream to make herself that much more alert. Paul felt their daughter's pres-ence in the house would force him and Cherry to be civil with each other. He did not want a scene. Paul poured two glasses of wine and slid one toward Cherry. His stomach twisted as he heard himself say to Cherry, Listen, there's something I need to tell you.

When Paul first got together with Cherry, he took my older sister, Juliet, and me to Spain for a vacation with Cherry and Cherry's two sons. The idea was to get acquainted, we were a blended family now. Cherry knew the area, she rented a house close to her brother's, the house was a short drive to the beach. In the rental house, Cherry and Paul took the master bedroom, and Cherry's sons were given the second, smaller bedroom. Juliet and I slept in the main room of the rental house on a pull-out couch. Every morning, we woke up pushed together, having rolled into the couch's soft centre, and Juliet would say, Back the fuck up, loser. Juliet was shaped like a Corvette, her hair in a braid like an extra spine, her tan lines stark and perfect like a ghost bikini. In the main room, we turned our backs to each other, pulled off our thin nightgowns, and rushed to get dressed before anyone came in. We were infected by loneliness. Walking the beach alone with my father one afternoon I asked him why he had left our mother. Women kept turning to get a second look at him. My father was about to become famous with his novel *Daughter*, and it was as if the women of Spain could feel his fame approaching. My father wore a bandana tied around his neck and sun-faded swim trunks. His skin refused to burn. He glimmered under the sun, a slightly mangled hunk of dark gold, and women touched him in passing with their eyes. Your mother just didn't excite me anymore, my father said to me that afternoon on the beach in Spain, and I felt exhausted by his answer the way I do now listening to poets read their poetry.

As Paul confessed to Cherry, and time passed without any word from him, the sky went a saturated blue, and it lowered itself, pushing downward against me. I got into bed. I tried to read the internet. Wes was at his studio. I was alone with my guilt. I did an image search of Eva. Eva at a regatta with her rowing team. Eva running in a garbage bag, trying to qualify for the lightweight boat. Eva and me at Paul's film premiere, her athletic body trapped in an expensive dress. I am adjusting something at her neckline, Eva's hands rest on my shoulders. We ignore the camera, eyes set on each other. *There is this to consider. There's Eva.* Eva and I were close. We were not held back by the fact that we lived in separate realities, by our age gap of twelve years. If anything, it was these differences that bound us. Eva was relieved by my presence. With me, there was nothing to prove or to win. I made art. I was a deadbeat. My hair was a mess. I had no real plan. But if Eva found out what I had known and concealed, she would feel duped, stung. Paul had given me a special role. To hide a cheat was to be a cheat. I was a liar. I was an actress which meant I was a con. She had fallen for a con. Cherry's sons would side with Eva. They had grown up with her, slept in the bedroom next to hers in Paul and Cherry's big house, Eva was their sister in a concrete way. It would be fine with me to lose them, we weren't close, they were bloodless and weird, I felt like a contamination in their presence. Cherry's sons wore pressed shirts and were always damp from the shower, they were serious and clean, their eyes hard as pills, a pharmaceutical blue, they had the same stare, the same driving need to win, I avoided them whenever possible. But Eva mattered to me. I knew how she would retaliate. Eva would stoke whatever relationship she had with our father to prove that she was the chosen daughter. Then she would enlist her steely mental discipline to turn her love for me in on itself. She would replace her love with a feeling equal in size and just as formidable. It would not be something so basic as hate, it would be something emptier, lighter, easier to live with, more practical and final. It would be neutrality.

I closed my laptop. I felt hypersensitive to the weight of the bedcovers, the crawl of my skin. My first play, *Margot*, had just been programmed for the upcoming fall season at the theatre where I was artist-in-residence, and I should have been celebrating. I should have been drunk with Ani. Instead, I thought only of Paul, I thought nervously about Paul. My nerves were like curtains of rain sweeping through my body. What had he said? Was Cherry kicking him out? Had he gone to Lee's? A motorcycle roared by. The wind kicked up, and the front window slammed shut. I could hear my neighbours next door, they were arguing, they never argued. I got out of bed, and went to the kitchen where I could hear them better. Maybe they weren't arguing. They were talking about me, making the case for what a desperate daughter I was, what a two-faced sister. I had a sordid contract with my father. I was obsessed with my childhood. I had never gotten over my childhood. Cherry had been cruel to me as a child, and I wanted to get back at Cherry, and so I guarded my father's secrets like a stash of weapons, waiting for the moment I could strike. Eva was collateral. I found a bit of wine in the fridge and despite the sourness, I stood in the fridge's rectangle of yellow light and I drank it. I held the neck of the empty bottle. I pressed my ear to the wall and listened. My neighbours' voices overlapped too much to pry apart. I would get what I deserved. The sky turned black, the moon was a skull. I checked my phone, nothing changed.

At the kitchen table, Paul told Cherry the affair began two years ago during his European tour for the film adaptation of *Daughter*. Lee was Paul's publicist and she travelled with him, took care of everything, his plane tickets, hotel rooms, dry cleaning, directions, currencies, media appearances, readings, signings, everything. She was a very caring person. In fact, Paul felt Lee lived for him, Paul was Lee's reason to live, she did not have much else in her life, her mother died when she was thirteen and her father died soon after, a brain aneurysm at the margarine factory where he worked, she had been sent to live with an aunt, but it had been a sterile environment for Lee, she had moved to the city, got her degree, landed an internship which became her job, her modest, low-paying job, but she was so good at it, she was assigned to Paul, and with Paul, she travelled the world, without Paul, she leased her furniture, and Paul worried that if he broke off with Lee, Lee might take her own life. Paul shocked himself with this last point. He heard his voice waver and cleared the swamp of acid from his throat. Sweat darkened the back of his dress shirt. Paul hated himself for this show of vulnerability. He glanced over at Cherry. The stern line of her mouth, the slope of her neck, she was still as a drawing. Cherry did not move. Paul was the one shifting in his seat, holding his head in his hands. Paul felt drilled into by Cherry's gaze. That detonating look. Cherry had radiant brown eyes, and she held Paul there like a toy. When his daughters from his first marriage visited, Cherry hid her copper pots in the trunk of her car and boxed her good linens. She did not want his daughters touching her fine things. She stuffed her jewellery into the toes of her old tennis shoes. When his daughters visited, they had to list any foods they consumed. Cherry defended herself and said the ledger was so she could properly replenish. Didn't Paul like the stocked fridge? The full pantry? Eventually, his teenage daughters brought their own meals. Eventually, his adult daughters stopped visiting altogether. Cherry's father had invented Styrofoam. Cherry was a Styrofoam heiress. She could fill their house with money. She could stack money from floor to ceiling in every room of their big house. Paul had never seen Cherry cry, not even after she gave birth to Eva. She fascinated Paul and disturbed him. Cherry knew very well who Lee was. She had met Lee a number of times, and felt Lee was not exactly a sophisticated machine. Cherry was tall with a striking, angular face. She was like a spire: erect, proud, lean. Lee was, in every way, her physical opposite. Like shined meat, Lee was pink and soft-edged, a supplicant. Cherry was an observant person, especially when it came to any interest in Paul. She had antennae for this sort of thing. She had completely overlooked Lee, and was surprised Paul had fallen for his publicist, and not one of the stars of the film. The stars were so sultry, so worshipful, it was almost embarrassing to watch them fawn over Paul. She could see why Paul felt worried that, without him, Lee might decide her life had no meaning. Paul was like the sun. Lee lived alone in public housing, watered the tomato plants on her windowsill, was about thirty years younger than Paul. She was suburban, awed by city life, had a basic education. It was not as if she were on her way to some grand thing. She was simple, a simple woman. Lee was an administrator. That was the sum total of Lee. Lee had no hold over the universe. The universe would discard her, starting with Paul.

Recently, Cherry had inherited an island four hours northeast of the city. Laid out on the table before Cherry and Paul, throughout their conversation about Paul's affair, was the blueprint for their island home. It would be built that summer. Cherry was working closely with the architect. She was overseeing every decision. The fate of the island had been deadlocked for years as Cherry's brother had contested the terms of their father's estate. Cherry's brother was petty, insecure. He had never learned to hide his hunger. Throughout the dispute, Cherry's mother had kept silent, which Cherry felt was the most spineless way to side against her. Cherry never looked at her mother again. Instead she penetrated the eyes of the arbiter and led him through the sure and efficient structures of her mind. She told him that one either honoured or betrayed *the will* of a man who no longer had a say in the matter. Cherry took on a widow's countenance and a widow's tone for she was the widow, her grief was a wife's grief, Cherry was the daughter and the wife, Cherry had been everything to her father. When Cherry was old enough she was the one to accompany her father to society events. Her mother walked just behind them outside of the photographers' frames. Cherry had a model's body though not a model's face. About Cherry's face, people used descriptors for a beauty they did not understand. This was Cherry's preference. Cherry did not want to be understood. As a woman, to be understood was to be possessed and conquered. Like Lee. Without commenting on the affair, without any acknowledgement of what Paul had just confessed to, Cherry updated Paul on the island home. She traced over the drawing with her long, elegant fingers. She told him that at every corner of the main house, she and Paul would have a view of open water. She told Paul to always look forward, never look back, and Paul was overwhelmed with gratitude, he felt his eyes sting, mistaking Cherry's comment to mean he'd been forgiven.

Paul told me about his affair with Lee when he was already deep into it, his every thought pervaded by her. I had moved back to the city and was newly living with Wes. I was trying to write my first play, but feeling beneath the endeavour. There was already a writer in the family and he was a titan. I took extra shifts at the bar, I was a minor character in my own minor life. I had met Lee. In my final year of theatre school, at the end of a dinner with Paul, Lee walked into the restaurant and Paul introduced us. I was in a bad frame of mind then, an anaesthetic state. I remember shaking Lee's hand, and not much more. Six months later, Paul told me his secret. We had not had a real conversation in years. Normally, we argued and misunderstood each other, and I saw myself through my father's eyes as volatile, emotionally disorganized, repellent. Until Lee, whenever Paul and I arranged to meet, I was late. It took me horrible amounts of time, horrible amounts of life to decide what to wear. Everything I put on looked cheap and dirty and ill-fitting. My apartment would be overturned when I left it, got on my bicycle and rode into a richer part of the city to meet my father who would have already ordered his meal, hungry and irritated by my lateness. My heart would beat violently in my chest, and I would feel self-conscious locking up my bicycle and making my way to his table. He would comment on my dress and my hair, my bag, which, to his eyes, would appear over-packed. He would make a joke at my expense and our tense visit would begin. This time, when I sat down and caught my breath, Paul said, I'm in love, I'm just so in love, and I don't know who else I can talk to. I need your help. And I listened to Paul like my life depended on it, I listened absorbingly, and with his every word, I felt myself expand. Cherry, Paul said, had become impossible to live with. Living with her, Paul said, was deadening. It was like life between novels. It was flat, dimensionless. There was no enchantment. She was so controlling. He could not take a shit without her leaving a memo about it. At that, we laughed like allies. My body pulsed with energy. The scales had fallen from Paul's eyes. *To be loved by your father is to be loved by God.* The first line of my play came to me. It was hard not to clap the air. Go on, I told Paul. There were notes taped all over the house, Paul went on. Cherry didn't have a bank account. She distrusted everyone. She had gotten into a fight with the neighbours over their backyard fence so now Paul had to skulk whenever he went outside to smoke. She wanted to sue her hairdresser. She was obsessed with Eva, and blamed Paul for Eva's eating disorder. Cherry said Eva deprived herself because Eva felt Paul favoured me and Juliet. Cherry said Eva had been born into an uneven love. Cherry said even though Paul denied it, one of us was obviously the inspiration for *Daughter*, and because of that, Eva could not begin to compete with us as we had been immortalized. You made your choice of favourite daughter in your work, Cherry said, now you must do so in your life. Jesus, Paul said, and then he laughed to himself. Anyway, it was so unpleasant, so stressful. He could not stand to be home so he made excuses to be on the road. With Lee, he was doing his best writing. She made him feel vital again. I'm in love, Paul said. The sex, Paul said. Then his face clouded over. Paul reminded me that Cherry had estranged herself from her mother. Cherry's mother had just died, and Cherry didn't go to her mother's funeral. She was a drinker, Paul said. Her pancreas. Soon after, a Rothko showed up on their front porch. Cherry felt her mother had given her the Rothko because she knew Cherry disliked Rothko. Cherry said people saw depth in Rothko but it was only searching. Searching does not make you great, Cherry said. Searching makes you the same as everyone else. People use the word *genius* for Rothko not to elevate his art but to elevate their own tastes. Cherry said Rothko killed himself because he knew he had reached his peak as a painter. That must have been hell, Cherry said, and she had the painting hung in their living room. Paul could hardly think about it, about who Cherry was. All these years after that disastrous trip to Spain, and Cherry still had not spoken to her brother. She still had not forgiven him for taking in me and Juliet after the incident with the garden hose, after we'd been forced to flee the rental house. Paul felt there was something wrong with Cherry, something cold and calculated he wanted neither to see nor understand. He was scared. He was scared to leave Cherry for the fallout. She would make his life a misery. She would sabotage his reputation, his work. She would turn Eva against him. As much as he had grown to care about them, or maybe it was tolerance, it was probably tolerance, Paul would be fine living without her sons. They accepted Paul because he was with Cherry, they were soldiers to Cherry, and upon her command, they would scrap him. But Eva was his daughter, and he could not stand to cause her any pain. I love Eva, Paul said. Twenty years ago, Paul said, when he left our mother, Natasha, when he left us, he was so young and selfish, he didn't know a thing. My reality was the only one I could see, Paul said. Lee has taught me so much. She has opened my eyes. She is tender. I feel such remorse for the pain I caused you. Paul stopped there, and he reached across the table for my hand which was warm and sure. Then, Paul told me that early into his relationship with Cherry, he had real misgivings. He was about to end it when Cherry told him she was pregnant, when Cherry got pregnant with Eva.

The day after Paul confessed his affair with Lee to Cherry, he called me and asked to meet for dinner. I can't get into it, Paul said over the phone, but it's important we talk. Things have escalated. I had waited up for his call the night before. It was late when Wes came through the apartment door. I got out of bed to greet him. Wes had been at his studio, he was under deadline. He told me I was shivering. I guess I'm cold, I said. Wes took off his jacket, hung it from my shoulders, got a glass of water. I followed him around. He asked me why I was gripping my phone like a grenade. Ha. I must have fallen asleep with it, I lied. I could not tell Wes about Paul. My father's presence in our relationship was already outsized. I didn't want to fight with Wes. He would tell me what I already knew. Focus on your work and not your father's psychodrama. I could not tell Wes that Paul's affair with Lee had filled me with an aggressive energy, I wrote my play during the course of his affair, as if one depended on the other, one powered the other, as if I did not write my play, but Paul's confidante did. Whoever she was. I kissed Wes's neck, his cheekbone, his mouth. I watched him undress, made a show of my tiredness, felt only my nothingness, and with Wes beside me, fell into a fitful sleep.

I met Paul for dinner at his favourite restaurant, and even though it was a cool spring night, we sat outside. A couple stopped by the table to say hello to Paul, and Paul motioned to me and said, This is my daughter Mona, Mona Dean, Mona is a playwright and an actress, she graduated from theatre school a couple of years ago, look for her name, she has a show on in the fall called *Margot*, and I stood and shook their hands, and the couple appeared amused and asked whether it was Margot as in Hemingway and I said yes, and they said well that seems fitting, and then they asked me which spelling I would use of her name, and I said the one on her gravestone. And then the couple told Paul we looked exactly alike. They could really see the resemblance. Once the couple had left the table, Paul told me that Cherry was very hurt. She'd hidden it at the time, but she'd been blind-sided by his confession. He didn't know if she was gathering her troops or what, but Cherry had told Eva about his affair with Lee. Oh no, I said. Then Paul said he was worried he had made an error in judgment. I asked what, what error in judgment. And fear entered my mind like a crow. Paul said when he was confessing to Cherry, he did not know if he was overcome with relief after so much lying or if he wanted Cherry to understand that the affair with Lee had arisen out of a larger problem, the problem of their broken family, the problem of their brokenness, it was not just the result of his self-centredness or vanity or greed or duplicity or lust or id or death complex or whatever you wanted to call it, his fatal flaw. In any event, Paul told Cherry some of the things I had confided to him during our period of extreme close-ness. It became a larger conversation, Paul said, and you were pretty central to it. Go on, I said, you'd better tell me ev-erything. Paul told Cherry every complaint, every slight I had divulged to him, every accumulated hurt. Paul told Cherry that I felt she toyed with love, by giving love and withholding love, and that only sick people manipulated others in this way. Paul told Cherry that I said she arranged their life in order to exclude me and Juliet from it, that excluding me and Juliet was her primary goal. She had never worked, so she could measure her worth only through her children. She had made Eva a star in Paul's eyes while poisoning his view of me and Juliet, we were jealous, disturbed, and played the victim the way our mother had, and because of Cherry's hateful campaign, he, Paul, my father, had missed everything, he had missed my entire life. All that had happened to me, all that I had done. Paul told Cherry that on the rare occasion I was invited into their home, for a birthday or a holiday, I was made to feel like vermin. Cherry belittled me. She insulted me. Juliet had an instinct for self-preservation. Juliet had moved to the other side of the world. I had told Paul in my litany of grievances that he was with Cherry out of fear, their marriage was intact only because of an implied threat, the implied threat being if he ever left her, Cherry would make his life a living hell. Paul relayed these things to Cherry who then went upstairs and relayed them to Eva.

Eva was fast asleep when her mother shook her awake and told her what had happened. Eva sat up, and cleared her eyes. She was upset for her mother, she could see Cherry felt humiliated by Paul's affair, it was difficult to watch her mother in pain. She had never seen her mother in pain before, but it was the fact that I had been Paul's confidante throughout his affair with Lee that Eva kept turning over and over in her mind. In meticulous detail, Cherry described my role as secret accomplice to Paul. Whatever unbearable blanks Paul had left Cherry to imagine, she filled in for Eva, embellishing ugly fact with uglier fiction, pegging me as the traitor not Paul. Cherry had to keep her household together. She had to aim the sharpened arrow of Eva's spite at me. Eventually, Eva told Cherry that because Paul teased her for being so unlike him, he called her a secluded person with a secluded heart, then by contrast lit up at the briefest mention of our names, she always felt that Paul preferred me and Juliet to her, and this betrayal only confirmed it. He lived with Eva but pined for us. No matter what she did, she was an afterthought to Paul. She was last born, last loved. Cherry was silent, and Eva took her mother's silence to be agreement. Eva felt a surge inside herself, it was the surge of recognition that came whenever her mother agreed with her. But she also felt in this moment the lonely pain of her observation about Paul. She was not his favourite. She was less than me, and she was less than Juliet. She was lowest in Paul's hierarchy. Eva wanted her father's love as much as she wanted her mother's love, and it was an open, hungry mouth on her open, hungry face. It was pathetic. Cherry was sitting on the side of Eva's single bed. It was late, and after too much wine, Paul had fallen asleep on the couch downstairs under the Rothko. Cherry had woken her daughter to tell her what had happened. She had crept upstairs in her stocking feet. Eva had an exam in the morning. Cherry could not stop herself. She needed the comfort only her daughter could provide. Her sons did not comfort her. She respected her sons, she admired their accomplishments, but they did not comfort her. She could not see into them the way she could see into Eva. Eva was like an open piano, she could see the steel cables, the other side of the keys. Until Eva was born, Cherry felt like an alien pretending to be a mother. Now she understood. She would kill for her daughter. There was some moonlight in the bedroom, and Eva looked at her mother's outline, she was like an apparition in the moonlight, Eva could feel her mother's intense stare. She loved her mother and it was her mother's love for her that was her source of energy. Even when Eva would become a mother herself, her love for Cherry would be her dominant and guiding feeling, it would propel her forward. Eva played a reel across her mind of the times we had spent together. The reel was too much like those sentimental movies where one of the sisters dies at the end. Eva would not be the sister to die at the end. When the reel finished, Eva's heart hardened against me. She told Cherry that despite my endearments, I had never been a true sister to her because, fundamentally, I had always wanted her parents' marriage to fail. Cherry agreed with her daughter. Eva felt the surge. Then Cherry pushed it one step further.

Your father told me that Mona said she loathes me. *Loathe*—Cherry drew out the word.

Loathe. That is such a murderous word.

Exactly, Cherry said to her daughter, exactly.

Our meals arrived. Sitting outside with my father at his favourite restaurant, after he had replayed the night, his confession to Cherry and Cherry's recruitment of Eva, I looked down at my plate. It was steaming. I felt cold and pulled my jacket on. It was a leather jacket, and in it, I felt like a cliché. The cliché of the wild daughter. My role as confidante to my father had given my life discernible shape, and now that shape was dissolving. Paul was pulling away. Something was actively converting inside him. Paul was switching course, going from one state to another, one side to the other. I could feel it as keenly as I could feel my own dissolution. I couldn't eat. Paul's eyes were blank as hardware. There was nothing in me he wanted or needed to see. I represented only his entanglements, his weak and lustful heart. I asked Paul how Lee was. He said he had no clue. He wasn't answering her calls because he didn't have anything to tell her. He said Lee was needier than he'd thought, and that was too bad. She's young, her entire life is ahead of her, Paul said impatiently, she can do whatever she wants. In silence, we both tried to stomach this lie. Paul ate mechanically. His body was stiff, it was the same stiffness that followed our arguments from before. He had gone from liquid to metal. I told Paul that Eva would never speak to me again, she would cut contact. I felt a tightness in my throat, the stinging pressure of rising tears. Paul did not respond. Rather he sat rigid in his chair then edged it away. I touched my face to be sure it was still there. His green eyes ignored mine. Deliberately, Paul studied the restaurant, the sidewalk, the street beyond. He behaved as if I were bothering him, as if I were a woman he didn't know lingering at his table while he was trying to have a quiet evening.

During our period of extreme closeness, I told Paul about the abortion I'd had at fifteen. He said I could have come to him for help at the time. He would have helped me. He looked wounded when he said that, and I knew he felt his comment to be true. I told Paul that I'd been raped by a guest director at theatre school, I didn't tell anyone when it happened, I was full of self-loathing, I was ashamed, I still hadn't told anyone, I'd told Ani about it and Wes knew, but not Natasha, not Juliet, and now the guy was a hotshot in LA, he was always in the tabloids shirtless and jogging like Shia LaBeouf. And Paul said angrily, who's Shia LaBeouf? I told Paul how at theatre school Wes had been Ani's boyfriend before me—until me, really. And to my betrayal of Ani, to this new information that I was also a cheat, Paul responded, we are more alike than we thought, Mona. Everyone aligns me with Juliet, but it's you and I who are closer in character. This was at the apex of our period of extreme closeness. We lifted our glasses and we hit them together, and Paul said, To you, my redeemer.

—

Now, at Paul's favourite restaurant, I wanted to tell him that
his fatal flaw was that he triangulated his relationships. He
always needed someone to be left out, to be kept in the dark.
Paul would tell me something and make me promise not to
tell anyone, not even Juliet. A few months into my role as
confidante to Paul, I told him he had to tell Juliet about his
relationship with Lee. I hated having a secret from Juliet, it
felt wrong, I was constantly lying to her by omission. Across
from me that cool spring night, Paul was finishing his dinner.
He said harshly, Aren't you going to eat? Paul was shunning
me. He did not want me there. My sadness depleted him.
And then Paul said, Juliet was right. The second I told Juliet
about the affair, she said, End it. I had a family, and despite
how badly you and Juliet had been treated by that family, I
needed to be a responsible husband and father. I needed to
man up. Paul said to me, I'm lucky. I'm so lucky to have a
level-headed daughter like Juliet. The server cleared our
plates. Now there was nothing to do but be alone together.
Paul checked his watch. He pushed his hands into his pockets,
felt for his keys, he was readying to go. He flagged the server
and paid. Paul told me he was going to try to work things out
with Cherry, she was a good person, and he wanted her forgiveness. Looking back on it, he and Cherry had had a good
life together. He told me I needed to work things out with
Cherry too. If I didn't, I would be making a big mistake.

That sounds like blackmail, I told Paul, don't blackmail me.

Don't get emotional, Paul said, the last thing I need is another outburst. When was I put in charge of everyone's feelings?

Then Paul said he probably would have found Lee boring in the long run. She was simple, a simple woman. And Eva, Paul said, Eva is so fragile. She has so much going for her, but she's always bursting into tears.

.   .   .

Two months after the dinner, Wes called Paul. I didn't know about the call. Wes called Paul from his studio where he had more privacy than in our one-bedroom apartment. He still needed to whisper into the phone as it was a shared studio, and there were a few artists around that afternoon. Paul picked up. He was surprised and happy to hear from Wes, he liked Wes, and Wes told Paul he didn't know what to do with me. How so, Paul said. Wes explained that I was in the final revisions of my play, *Margot*, maybe Paul had forgotten about *Margot*, my professional debut, the theatre had made me artist-in-residence which was a big deal, they had given me an office to write in, but after my dinner with Paul, the night Paul decided to break off with Lee and mend things with Cherry, I had stopped showing up. There was a reading of *Margot* next week, and everyone was waiting on the latest draft of the script. The show was supposed to open the fall season. My face was painted on the side of the building, my face covered the entire side of that downtown building. Now the theatre was considering pulling the show. It was a one-woman show, and I was the one woman, and I was spending entire weeks in our bed. Wes told Paul he didn't know how to help me. He was really worried. He had been raised in a normal family in a normal house by normal parents. Paul's life was like some vicious wilderness program in which everyone was a lion, but I had to be a gazelle. Paul did not understand his power over me and my love for him. Or maybe he did understand it, and he just wasn't careful with it, and that was so much worse. Paul deserted me when I was eleven, and I had modelled my view of myself in response to that desertion. And Paul kept leaving me over and over again. He kept breaking my heart, and that was really ruining things for me, and for us. Paul interrupted to ask Wes whether he was done yet with his guilt trip, and Wes said, No, no, I'm not done. Then Wes told Paul he was going to propose to me, and he was not going to ask Paul for his permission, even though he knew Paul would expect it. Then he told Paul not to contact me unless it was with an apology. Paul said he didn't like to be threatened. Paul said, Don't ever threaten me again or you'll be sorry, and then he slammed down the phone on Wes.

. . .

Lying in our bed, I thought of everything that had gone wrong, and where I had left myself exposed.

Wes tried to reason with me. He said, But your face is already painted on the side of the theatre, and I said the theatre could just paint over my face. Wes said, Don't you care, and I said, Yes, I do care, I just can't do anything about my caring right now. Steady crying. I said a few more things, I said Paul can just paint over my face with Eva's, and Wes said, Why are you talking like that, do you think this is a joke, and I said, I'm sorry, the more pain I'm in the funnier I get, you know that.

I do. Mona, please, Wes said. And then under his breath, he said, Please don't let your father sabotage this too.

Wes paced and tried to settle himself at the end of our bed. He arranged himself like a horse on furniture. He was lanky and never quite fit in a room. Wes had explained song construction to me. He said, You have the verses and you have the chorus, but then you have the bridge, and everyone thinks the bridge, because it is called *the bridge*, the bridge is going to *bridge* one part of the song to the next part, but it's a departure. The bridge is an entirely different thing. The bridge of a song is composed separately from the song. It's a separate thing, produced elsewhere. You can edit a song and have all these components and move them around however you want. And then you *add* the bridge. The bridge, it's just this whole other thing.

—

Wes was my bridge.

I pushed aside the bedsheet and leaned against the wall. Wes was holding an electric fan, looking for the socket. A thin film of sweat glistened on his skin. He was wearing my satin robe. His forearms protruded from the sleeves, the sash was knotted too high across his chest like gift wrapping. I told Wes he had John the Baptist's body. I told him, there is a sculpture of John the Baptist in the museum garden, and every time I see that sculpture, I want to fuck it. It's a Rodin. Bronze. Wes dropped my satin robe, went dead still, extended an arm and parted his lips as if in sermon.

We had slow, hard sex against the kitchen counter. The metal rim dug into the small of my back, I could feel it against the base of my spine. My legs were tight around Wes's centre and he was deep inside my body. After, we opened the freezer door and let the freezer smoke cool us. Every light was off in the apartment. In the dark, Wes stood behind me with his hands on my hipbones and then on my breasts. I felt his cock twitch. We lay down, pressed our faces to the cold linoleum and looked at each other. Outside, heat lightning flashed in intervals. It's like we're being photocopied, I said to Wes. He smiled. I told Wes I had started to dream in auto-tune. Since this whole mess with Paul, whenever I speak in a dream, I am auto-tuned. Sorry to raise Paul right now, I told

Wes. Everything in my head is combining without scale. Wes asked me what I thought the message of the dream was, and I told him, I think it's pretty straightforward. The message of the dream is to be a more regulated woman. Then I told Wes the message was not being issued by my subconscious, but by Paul's. Paul had infiltrated my subconscious.

Paul is the third person in our relationship, Wes thought to himself, lying on the kitchen floor opposite Mona. Not Ani. Early on, there had been so much focus on Ani. Mona beat herself up over Ani when Ani was made of a different material. Ani was fine. Wes remembered the night he first met Paul. He and Mona were still living out of boxes when Paul called to invite them to dinner at the house. It would be casual, Paul said, Cherry was out of town. Paul had not yet told Mona about Lee. That saga was still to come. After she hung up, Mona said to Wes, The only thing Cherry taught me was to hate myself. Wes was upset by the remark. Mona was half leaning out the front window of the apartment, smoking. Don't look so horrified, she said back to Wes. Then she described Cherry's harassment of her as more comedic than anything, though it never felt that way at the time. When Wes said it sounded like Paul made Mona his human shield, sacrificing her for his own comfort, Mona got furious. She told Wes that his outrage toward Paul made her feel inadequate, like she hadn't done enough to defend herself. Wes had never even met her father and already he was judging him. Then Mona withdrew. She laughed to herself, and under her breath, she said, It's just how Paul is, you'll see.

The following night, heading to dinner, Wes felt like he was heading to a riot. Wes was in an aroused, fighting mood. But Paul's presence tranquilized him. Paul opened a bottle of wine, made easy conversation, he showed Wes some of the art in the house and whenever Wes made a comment, Paul complimented him on his insight. Wes wondered if his comments were of a higher quality than usual. The house was one of those endless, rambling structures that should have belonged to the public. Walking through it with Paul, Wes felt they were on the same side, like Paul did not live in the house, like he was the tour guide. They sat at the kitchen table and ate fancy takeout from Styrofoam containers. Wes had read *Daughter* before he went to theatre school, long before he had ever heard the name Mona Dean. He had read the novel twice, both times in a single sitting, as if reading the book lay outside of his control. Now, across from Paul, Wes felt Paul had the same magnetism as the book. Wes glanced over at Mona. She looked perturbed. Wes reached for her hand under the table. He wanted to comfort her, but Paul was asking him a question. Wes's answer could lead him into the nucleus of himself, he needed to hear it. Mona excused herself and was gone for what seemed like a long time. Wes started to clear the table. Paul looked down at the mess and told Wes, Leave the cleanup. He put his palm on Wes's back and steered him out into the garden to share a cigar and drink some Scotch. Wes could feel the pond water in the night air. It's the perfect temperature, Paul remarked, reading his mind. But also like an unfinished basement, Wes said, and Paul laughed. He gripped Wes's arm, and there was something erotic in his grip. Wes knew he was in a game, but not which one. It was clear he and Paul needed each other. Wes was in a period of transformation or maybe it was an identity crisis. He had graduated from theatre school feeling pissed off and like a pawn. Despite the overblown attention he got for his portrayal of Hamlet, the write-ups and the offers, the whole thing when Keanu Reeves came to the show, he had immediately quit acting and turned to installation art. He had destroyed his phone and basically exited society. Wes was telling this to Paul who was listening intently. Paul said he understood what it was to blow up one life for another. He'd done it himself and it took balls. They laughed as a way of changing the subject. Laughter was atomization. Mona said this and did this all the time. Paul told Wes that he had deviated from what was expected of him. It might make him unpopular, but he should stay the course, it would be worth it. Wes's own father had loved him from a good, cold distance, plainly and steadily. Wes pictured his mother still sleeping in his father's shirts. Wes felt he had been with Ani for those couple of months because of a single, sad conversation about dead fathers. It had been agonizing to play Hamlet, whose father visited his son as a ghost, giving him critical instruction from the afterlife. Wes had experienced the finality of his father's death like a door slammed shut, he could not even imagine what lay on the other side, whereas Ani's father sent her signs, like bats in the daytime, which told Ani what to do next and who to be. Wes wanted to get closer to his father's spirit. Wes knew that his father would think his pivot into art was indulgent and vain, but he would never have told him so. He certainly wouldn't glorify it the way Paul was. Paul coughed and it was an alarming sound. Wes wanted to ask Paul if he was okay, but he didn't want to insult him. He was Paul Dean. Paul crushed the end of his cigar into a butter dish, and coughed again more standardly. Wes pretended not to notice the noises Paul's body was making. Paul was in his sock feet, his jeans belted, some grease spots on his dress shirt. He was refilling Wes's glass. Not necessary. Wes was drunk, his clothes were drunk, his drunkenness was total. He wanted to smash something or go to sleep. Paul's pouring was inaccurate. He was the sort of man to deform shampoo bottles. Things were not happening at the right speed. There was reverb after every sound. Had Wes's father been speaking to him this whole time and he had been so caught up in himself that he had missed it? Wes's eyes grew hot. He felt like his face was being blowtorched. He needed to run his hands through Paul's hair. No, he needed Paul to run his hands through his hair. He needed to be touched and loved by Paul. Tell me more, Paul was saying to Wes when Mona came through the sliding door.

After the dinner, Wes asked Mona if she was up for walking home. He had had too much to drink and the aftertaste of the cigar in his throat sickened him. Paul and Cherry's house backed onto a public park, the massive pond lying black and still between the house and the park. Wes led Mona into the park and down to the pond. They stripped off their clothes, hung them from a tree branch and walked into the water. The moon was high. Wes had learned to swim late. He was not frightened of water but what moved beneath it. Maybe his father was a hologram in a golf shirt with a new wife and he and his mother were wasting their time being sad. Wes forced himself under the water. When he surfaced, his breath was short and he was looking directly at Paul and Cherry's big house. The lights were still on. What was Paul up to? He was with another woman. Wes was sure of it. Paul fed off people. The woman would intuitively clear the table. That was why Paul had told Wes to leave the cleanup. She would wash the butter dish. Wes peered over at Mona, on her back, her naked body floating. She was detached from Wes, inside her own thoughts. She was the moon on the water. Wes could drown and she wouldn't notice. It was a relief to be ignored. When Mona was writing, she was apart from him. He needed her apartness because it gave him his own. It was like a pact between them, as if they'd halved a drug. Wes watched

Mona's rib cage moving in and out. At the dinner, Paul had turned his attentions to Mona only when she mentioned she was writing a play. It was not going very well, she told Paul, but she wasn't ready to kill it just yet. Paul's reaction was over the top. It was like he went from prime time to reality television. He praised Mona, called her a visionary. Hardly, Mona said, embarrassed. Wes could see the strategy at work. Paul viewed Mona as a competitor, he was threatened by his daughter, she was edging into his territory, and his praise was meant to paralyze her. Wes came up for air. Was he gasping? He was gasping. He found the pond bottom and stood. The ankles and the neck were the most vulnerable parts of the human body. He tried not to picture *Night of the Living Dead*. Mona's eyes were closed. She was motionless on the water. His relationship with her had been some kind of delivery. It had been the delivery of himself. Being with Mona was like coming to life, and Wes nearly said this to her, but held back. She knew. Devotion was so relaxing. A lot could be left unsaid. Talking was like housework. Sex was the opposite. The lights were being switched off in Paul's house. The tour guide was going to have some fun. Paul cheated to stay alive. Wes saw that he had played a part for Paul. Their exchange seemed heartfelt at the time, but it was put on. Paul had played the wise, renowned writer to Wes's young, searching artist. He had adjusted himself to gain entry to Wes, to download Wes, and it was this ability to gain entry that made Paul a great writer, but a questionable person.

Wes and Mona dressed and with their hands clasped made their way out of the noiseless park and into the guts of the city. Still wet from the pond, Mona's dress clung to her body, her skin was slick. They were standing at a stoplight, waiting to cross, when Wes asked, What is it?

Nothing.

Mona.

She pulled an object from her dress pocket. It was a necklace. Mona pinched the pearl necklace at one end and let it hang from her fingertips. She said she knew it was fucked up, but whenever she entered that house and saw how she and Juliet had been erased from Paul's life, she felt driven to hurt Cherry. She did not even want the necklace, she was saying to Wes, but she was keeping it, the pearl necklace was hers. Then she said to Wes, Surely you hate me a little now, and Wes said he could never hate her, he could only love her. Please get used to it, Wes said.

.   .   .

Can you rearrange your soul? Can you make your soul sanitized, vacant, and neutral, can you make your soul beige and blank like a room at the Days Inn?

I asked myself this question and the answer was no.

.   .   .

When my father left for good, I watched him and Juliet cry in each other's arms. They were standing just inside our unlit garage. I was close by in the yard. I was eleven nearly twelve, I hadn't gotten my period yet. They didn't know I was there, loose and alone in the night. My sister was angry and beautiful like the ocean. I remember feeling not excluded from their love, but outside of it, and seeing then that my sister's job would be my father, and my job would be my mother. Natasha. Losing twenty, I don't know, thirty pounds from an already slender frame, getting home from work and going straight to the basement to cry.

At the hospital, my mother's stomach was pumped. She was stripped and led to an empty room. Even though it was summer, she was wearing three overcoats when she was admitted. Her hairpins were taken, her shoelaces, her lighter. The nurses took her three overcoats and gave her a single blanket, and then they instructed her to keep her hands on top of the blanket, where they could see them, and my mother said, What am I going to do, strangle myself? My mother told the doctors she had never felt so cold and the cold was her grief.

I know this story because my mother told it to me. We were in my mother's bathroom when she told me the story of her suicide attempt. By then I was twelve, I still hadn't gotten my period. We had just gone to the steak place near our house, we agreed the steak was always shaped like Florida, we would stare at the cooked meat, pick at the fries, come home. It was tough to be home. A painter I love does these big paintings of rooms, the painter is my closest friend, Ani, the rooms are empty, but animated. A book left open, a drink half-finished, a lamp left burning. The painter's rooms appear as if someone has just exited the frame. My father had just exited the frame. My mother told me the story of her suicide attempt as she was sitting on the closed toilet seat in her bathroom. I was in the bath, trying to still myself, but it was hard to be inside my scrawny body, my body felt infested like I had a mouse running through my limbs or some larger, slower animal I had been charged with hiding. I asked my mother if I could try her cigarette. She passed it to me. Soon, I would write my first play. My mother told me what it was like to be under psychiatric watch. The nurses say your name every chance they get because your name is like a flare, and it leads you back to yourself, the self that lives and has reason to live. Still, the days and nights feel thin, my mother said to me in her bathroom. Difficult to grasp and to get through.

.　.　.

You're always more unreal to yourself than other people are—Ani quoted Marguerite Duras. I told Ani my fear that nothing would ever grow inside my body. Ani said she wished she knew how to comfort me, but fear was fear. She pulled her smooth hair up into a bun. Ani said she felt like in that moment she understood everything. She said eyes, ears, and teeth, they don't last. Ani wore a pink slip with a T-shirt over it. She had cut the T-shirt off at the waist. The T-shirt read *Just Do It*. I said to Ani, What is life? And Ani said, Just do it.

.   .   .

I told Ani that when things are bad with Paul, I replay my childhood on a continual loop.

Your version of screening home movies, Ani said.

.   .   .

It was a large room, tiled and serene like the morgue. Juliet and I were in the guest room of Cherry's brother's place in Spain. We were too wound up to sleep. Earlier, Cherry had sprayed me with a garden hose and screamed, Just drown. *Just drown*, I said to Juliet in the unfamiliar dark. It is pretty funny considering we were right beside the ocean. By funny, you mean serious, Juliet replied. *Just drown*. It is pretty serious considering we were right beside the ocean.

After Spain, Juliet refused to go on the next summer holiday. She said to me, What are you even thinking? Cherry rented a vacation house on an island off Cape Cod for two weeks. After a bad first week, I moved in with a friend I had made on the mainland. She was called Ani. Ani lived with her mother, Marilyn. Ani's father had died the summer before of a heart attack, and Ani had been alone with his dead body. At first, she said, the change was very subtle. One morning, Paul showed up at Ani's house. I could see him take in the scene, the cat, Minister, the broken clocks, the dishes piled high in the sink, Marilyn, braless. Bras as bookmarks, bras in the oven. Paul thanked Marilyn for having me and then, overhearing a song on the radio, he opened his arms and Marilyn walked into them. Paul and Marilyn slow-danced in the entryway, moving only as much as they had to. You never told me, Ani's breath was hot in my ear, your father was such a babe. When the song ended, Paul extricated his body from Marilyn's and took me aside. He said that the night before, he had gotten into a fight with Cherry. He needed to go to the mainland to work, he had to turn in his final edits for *Daughter*. In the vacation house, Cherry had held their baby, Evangeline, in one arm and Paul's revised manuscript in the other. After a bitter back and forth, Paul got his manuscript from Cherry, he took the motorboat in to the mainland, and called in his edits from a pay phone. Once his work was finished and Paul went to return to the island, he found the motorboat was gone. Cherry had taken the motorboat. She had roped it to the second boat that came with the rental and towed the motorboat back to the island. She had left Eva and her sons with the nanny, driven in when she knew Paul wouldn't see her, and left Paul without a way back. There was a rowboat docked at the pier and Paul decided to take it not knowing who the rowboat belonged to or whether it was seaworthy. Water is always bigger when you are in it, Paul said, what was I trying to prove? He said he probably got into the rowboat to see if Cherry had tampered with it, to see if she had it in her.

I was in the back seat of the SUV between Cherry's glossy sons. When they bumped against me, they felt like hard plastic. Get a life, I said to Cherry's sons, and I meant it. We were driving home from Cape Cod. Paul hit the power lock. In the front row of the SUV was the baby, Evangeline, facing us in her car seat, and beside her, facing forward, the baby's nanny, Destiny. I knew Destiny watched Brian De Palma films with the baby. She kept the volume low and the baby turned away from the screen, but when Paul and Cherry were out, Destiny was watching *Dressed to Kill* with the baby. It was clear Paul and Cherry had made their peace. My father switched out selves like slides in a carousel. In the rear of the SUV, I took out my retainer, put it in my pocket and fell asleep. I dreamed about Bill Clinton. In my dream, Bill Clinton had two dicks. Later, when I told Ani about the dream, she said, Not a dream. In my dream, Bill Clinton was supine in a white shirt, red tie and grey suit, grinning with his zipper down and his dicks out. He was a happy man, a doubly happy man, and he wanted me to touch him, didn't I want to touch his two dicks? We pulled off the main highway onto a secondary highway, and stopped at a roadside diner for lunch. I was in my bathing suit and jean shorts, the waistband of my jean shorts was folded over, this was how Ani and I dressed that summer. I was twelve and a half. I went to the bathroom in the diner, my bathing suit was wet with blood, blood filled the toilet bowl. I made a pad out of toilet paper and tied my hoodie around my waist. The walls of the bathroom were covered in forest wallpaper, the trees moved when I studied them, the walls pulsed, and I was a sovereign being. When my father was alone at the cash, I went up to him and said, Please don't tell Cherry, but I need money, I need to go to a drugstore, I got my period. My father told me he didn't know what to do. I told him it was okay because I knew what to do. I said, Please don't tell Cherry, and I told him again to please give me some money so I could get what I needed. My father appeared completely lost. He went back to our table by the window, and he told Cherry I got my period. Cherry had Eva in her arms. Cherry looked at her baby and then at me, and she sniped, Do you want a diaper?

Paul was resting his elbow on top of the open driver's-side door, he had his hands cupped around his mouth, and he was yelling my name. Paul had pulled onto the shoulder of the secondary highway, his new family belted inside the SUV. I had left the roadside diner and I was running. There was a steep drop from the shoulder to flat land that then jutted upward and thickened into a forest. Paul reached in and shut off the engine. He yelled my name at my back.

While Natasha asked Paul about the cuts and bruises all over my arms and legs, I brushed by her and into the house like a beaten cat. Natasha was standing in the front door frame in a Y shape, as if she were holding up the house, in her white silk dressing gown, her skin like poured milk, smoking a Colt. Paul was dropping me off. Natasha was blocking Paul's entry. She was transmitting hurt. About my cuts, Paul shrugged and said, She threw a fit, Tash, she walked into a forest. Then he gazed at Natasha, her face was like a silent film, everything was being communicated by her eyes, she used to sing that Pretenders song, *I'm special, so special*, her body was backlit in the doorway, she had gotten so thin, where had all that flesh gone, and the house beyond her, the house that had sheltered him for so many years, then Paul turned away from Natasha, saying, There are certain things I am just not equipped to handle.

.   .   .

I hear night sky as nice guy.

.   .   .

The first time I had sex I got pregnant.

.   .   .

For my tenth birthday, Paul, Natasha, Juliet and I went to a small cabin north of the city. The cabin belonged to my father's editor, Judd. Judd was also my godfather, and he gave us the cabin for my birthday weekend. It was winter. My father, sister and I skied the trail around the lake while Natasha stayed in the cabin and made my birthday cake. When we got back from our ski, Paul lit a fire in the fireplace and the cabin instantly filled with smoke. We opened the windows and propped open the front door. My father doused the fire while my sister, mother and I stood outside, watching my father bat the smoke. My father discovered the flue was closed, he had forgotten to open it before setting the fire, he assumed it would be open, Judd had told him there was a maintenance guy and the maintenance guy would get everything ready. My father stood there with his hands on his hips. Then something dropped from the chimney into the fireplace, kicking up a cloud of ash. My father saw that a family of birds had built their nest in the chimney. We had incinerated the birds. My father collected the charred birds in his hands, he looked back at the three of us in the high snow in our turtlenecks and birthday crowns. What I did not know then was that Cherry was renting a cabin close by, in the same compound. Before we sat down to dinner, my father went for a walk, he did this often, we thought nothing of it, he was always dealing with his head, having to unlock something. My father was getting to know Cherry's sons, he appreciated their composure and he credited Cherry with it. She had gravitas. More and more, Paul's world with us felt chaotic. His last novel, the one he published just before my tenth birthday, had been met with middling reviews. He had yet to deliver his bestseller, *Daughter*. Cherry had tracked my father's career and told him he was stalling, something was holding him back, if he did not deal with what was holding him back, he would never hit his mark, he would just be another hobbyist. My father was not where he wanted to be, and he associated Natasha, Juliet and me with his feeling of failure. It was a problem of ascension, Cherry told my father, he just could not ascend with us.

· · ·

When your father exits the frame, you start to think, *I must not be enough*.

· · ·

47

Ani opened and closed the hood of her sweatshirt like an aperture. Then she combed her rough fingertips through my hair and sang "Addicted to Love." When I told Ani that Wes called Paul my Original Sorrow, Ani said, I'll make you a perfume called Original Sorrow. Perfume is tears anyway.

. . .

Ani described herself as a very secure painter. Like a lighting effect, she had watched her father's soul shimmer in the room where he died, but no one had taught her more about painting than Marie Kondo. The whole joy thing, Ani summarized, knowing what to leave out.

. . .

The landline in Wes's studio is big and beige and attached to the wall. Along its receiver it has a piece of masking tape, on which, written in large black letters, are the words *DIRECT LINE TO YOUR PAST.*

. . .

I must not be enough. The thought grows into a defect, and no amount of love can make the defect go away. It is only the father's return that can make the defect go away, and despite knowing this will never happen, you still hold out hope.

.   .   .

We were in the ravine. I had my jeans and underwear pushed down to my ankles, my combat boots would have taken too long to unlace. The nice guy smelled like lighter fluid. I was lying on his open trench coat looking up at the night sky when the nice guy opened the tricky condom packet with his teeth.

When we broke up a month later, the nice guy said the only thing we were good at was treating each other badly. He left wilted flowers on my doorstep. He slapped my face on a moving train. I would see him around, and I would ignore him even when he tried to speak to me, even when he yelled at me and called me Psycho. I saw around him, I saw through him. I never told him about the pregnancy. What could he do? How could he help me? It's not like he could take it back.

.   .   .

The abortion doctor entered the procedure room hobbling. Then she sneezed, and it sounded like *Fuck you!* Excuse me, she said. I was fifteen. She was in a boot cast. She explained that she had two mastiffs, big dogs, she was going down the stairs to check their water when she fell. She said she heard the ankle before she felt it.

—

In the waiting room, I was given the option of having Juliet there with me for the procedure, but I said, No, I'll be fine. Juliet and I read the magazines that were fanned out on the low circular table in the middle of the room. Apparently, our lungs are mostly on our backs, I said to Juliet. News to me, she said. Then I was handed a clipboard and asked to fill out the paperwork. I couldn't remember my name and address, Juliet took over. I was led to a changing room. Maybe we underestimate the term *changing room*, I said to the attendant. The attendant told me to put my things in a locker and get into a gown. I held the gown against my body. Other way, the attendant said, it ties at the back. Why do they call it a gown? I asked the attendant, but by then she was gone.

.   .   .

Ani said, When I die, I want to be left in the forest, I want to be placed at the base of a very large tree and then I want the animals to go at me. Take my eyes, take my organs. I want the birds to go at me, the big game. A stag would be ideal.

.   .   .

After the abortion, Juliet and I took the southbound train home. The train sped through the tunnels, it shrieked against the tracks. I had a paper bag in my lap, painkillers, maxi pads, instructions for what to do if I hemorrhaged. I couldn't get my perceptions clear, and figured I was probably still high from the sedative. I had gone from pregnant to unpregnant in a matter of minutes. *It will be hard to make peace with this*, I thought to myself, and then I thought being stoned has made me clichéd. Now I can rely on the easy phrases of others, I don't have to come up with anything original. The abortion was the abortion of my originality. I looked down, and saw the change had already begun. I was dressed in nice, trendy clothes. A nice sweater with nice pants under a nice jacket with nice shoes. Then I remembered I was wearing Juliet's clothes. That morning, I'd said to my sister, I just don't want to be myself today.

You're my emergency contact, I said to Juliet in the train car, and she put her arm around me. Love in my body felt different from the love I read about. Love in my body felt like getting knifed. A nearby passenger asked Juliet if I was her daughter, and Juliet said to the passenger, She's my sister, what the fuck is wrong with you? And then she said to me, What the fuck is wrong with people?

We got home, went into the basement, turned out all the lights and watched *Blue Velvet*. Upstairs, Natasha sat in the kitchen with Paul's editor, my godfather, Judd. After Paul left us, Judd started showing up with his arms full of greasy takeout. He would park his sedan on the curb in front of the house and leave his flashers on. When Natasha opened the door, Judd would always say, I'll only stay a minute.

A few weeks later, I was back at the birth control clinic. I told the counsellor that I was still pregnant, I could feel the baby, the baby's heart was like the blades of a helicopter and they were rotating inside my abdomen. The counsellor explained that the pulse I was feeling in my abdomen was a major artery. An abortion is final, the counsellor said. But it's not final, I said, to abort is to stop, but not to end, the baby might have been stopped, but the baby is not ended in me.

.   .   .

It's your heart only. It's only your heart.

.   .   .

With the bluntness of a flipped switch, I jolted my head out of the past and back into the present. It was now August in the city. I could practically grope the air. The reading of my play, *Margot*, was the following day and I felt sick with anticipation. Ani stood behind me. We were in front of my bathroom mirror. I was in a rain poncho and Ani wore latex gloves. She was bleaching my dirt-brown hair to match Margot Hemingway's blond. Taped all around us were film stills of Margot Hemingway. Ani circled the dye brush in its bowl and began painting the frost-blue mixture over my hair. I could feel myself trying to break Ani's focus, enter her psyche, get her onto my uneven plane. Margot hated her sister Mariel. Mariel responded by beating Margot at the thing she loved most, acting. Mariel woke up one night to Margot's hands around her throat. Why had Shakespeare not called the play *King Lear's Daughters*? What was Eva up to right now? She would be leaving the city soon. She would be packing for school, purging her mind, cutting our relationship down to nothing. When I called Eva, she did not let the calls go unanswered. Instead, she picked up, and after a breath, disconnected. *Eva?* She loved to leave me stranded with my question. I shifted my anxious body in the chair. Be still, Ani said. I told Ani about this woman on the internet whose motto was *my life is my art is my problem*, and I said shouldn't it be *my life is my problem is my art*. No, Ani said, that's capitalist. Ani pulled off the gloves. She was done. We sat on the sill of the open front window and let the blond dye set. I listened to the waves of Ani's breath. Sometimes when Ani entered Wes's and my apartment, I could feel her try to calibrate her love for me. I wanted to tell Ani, don't bother. Our love began when we were twelve. We were too young at its formation to ever get ahead of it. There was no turning back.

Ani left. Wes was at his studio. In the empty apartment, I felt combustible. Only working released the pressure. I sat down with my script. I would note the beats and modulations,

I would get my nerves under control. I was Paul Dean's daughter making her writing debut. The attention would be forensic. I had to be nothing short of a diamond bending the light. A week before, I had called the artistic director of the theatre and appealed to him. I told him I had hit a bad patch, but was out of it now. I had come to my senses. I had even more to give the project. I had heard that he was close to swapping out my show, announcing the replacement for *Margot*, but he wouldn't have to. The reading kicked off rehearsals. The script would be rehearsal ready. I will deliver, I told the artistic director, my voice was low and firm and leading, yet when I hung up, I saw that I was shaking. I had lied. I had lied in order to trap myself into making the statement true. I could not lose this show.

I was making a note in the margin beside my opening line, *To be loved by your father is to be*—when my phone buzzed. It was Cherry. Something must have happened to Paul. Cherry and I had never spoken on the phone so Paul must be injured or maybe he was ill. Paul got drunk, stumbled down the stairs, punctured a lung. In his distraction he had crashed the car, sliced off a finger. Or maybe he had done an about-face and left Cherry for Lee, Cherry didn't know where Paul was, she needed my help locating him, without his blood pressure meds, Paul's heart could seize. He could die. Surely, he had phoned me, his confidante. When I asked Cherry if Paul was alright, whether something had happened to Paul and that was the reason behind her call, Cherry said, I do need to tell you something, Mona, but it should be in person and it will have to be now. I'm in the sculpture garden.

I sat next to Cherry with space enough between us for a third person. Cherry said, Look who's a blond. Despite the thick air, the white sun, I shuddered, then disintegrated into the glare of the sun, into the hot pavement of the sculpture garden. I ran my hands through my bleached hair, hid them in the pockets of my black dress, then folded my hands like cheap porcelain across my lap. Cherry stared straight ahead. She studied the large, contorted lead sculpture directly across from us. It was of a nude, armless woman who at first appeared to be in ecstasy, but on closer inspection had been stabbed in the back. Cherry's hair was short and brushed off her face. She wore a white dress, plain and pressed as a sheet of paper, her black purse strap cutting across her breastbone. At Cherry's neck was a thin gold chain that glinted like an accusation. A year into the affair with Lee, Paul asked me to meet him at a jeweller. He wanted to get something for Lee. Something in line with his feelings. It could not be too extravagant. He had me try on the assorted necklaces, angle my head this way and that, let my hair down as Lee wore hers long. Paul settled on a thin gold chain. Cherry wore the same chain now. After Paul confessed to Cherry, he must have returned to the jeweller, debated necklaces, and determined that the understated chain would understate the affair. If Paul overdid the chain, the implication would be that he had that much more to be sorry for. I asked Cherry again if something had happened to Paul, was Paul alright, and she dismissed my question with her hand, Paul is fine. I moved to leave the metal bench when Cherry grabbed me by the wrist and said, But Eva.

Cherry said she knew I felt I was close with Eva. I cut Cherry off to say that I was close with Eva, this was both a feeling and a fact. Then Cherry, in her lucid way, eviscerated me. She told me the closeness I felt to Eva was not a reality but an imitation of reality. I had manufactured my closeness with Eva in an effort to win over Paul. Everything I did was in pursuit of Paul. My selfhood belonged to Paul. Eva was a supporting character in my show for Paul. In being a good sister, I was demonstrating that I was a good daughter. Was I a good daughter? Cherry asked. What a desolate question— Cherry made this comment more to herself. She glanced down at the collapsed bag by my feet and murmured, All those nasty things you said about me to Paul. I don't love you. You don't love me. Should we just sit here and cry about it? Then Cherry's eyes went from the sculpture to the sky to scanning me, to peeling back my skin, and she said, Paul and I have come to a decision. You will no longer see your father without me there.

—

Cherry and I sat in silence. Cherry willed the silence. Above us, cloud cover rolled in and rendered us grey and motionless. Cherry willed the sky to change. It was my turn to speak and all I could hear was the shallow rumble of my breath inside the dumb shell of my body. I could not compose my body. I could not compose my thoughts, the cable between my thoughts and their expression had snapped. *You will no longer see your father.* A seagull landed near my feet and made its plaintive cry. The seagull nosed my bag. I picked up my bag and pulled it protectively to my chest then swatted the air with my hand. I was violent toward the seagull when it was Cherry whom I wanted to die. I did not just beg for Cherry's death, I tried to will it into reality, knowing that even from death, Cherry would reach across the veil to turn my fantasies against me. There was no killing Cherry. I thought of Cherry's father. His motorboat had been found circling the water off the island he'd just bought for his daughter. The accepted truth was suicide. Cherry insisted it was an accident. Her father was thrown into a rough sea. Only an idiot would say otherwise. Cherry held press conferences, sat for intimate interviews. Cherry poised in a black suit and pearl necklace before the scrum of microphones on the dock of the marina after her father's lacerated body had washed up on the shore. Maybe it was true. Maybe the woman you are is the woman your father wants you to be.

—

I thought back to when Eva visited me at theatre school. She made the three-hour trip to watch my final performance in *Hamlet*. After the show, with Ani and the cast gathered onstage, Eva got drunk for the first time. She was a moody drunk. At the end of the night, we lay in my small bed. Between her hiccups, Eva said, We are identical when I am drunk. We laughed until we fell asleep. The following morning, I came out of the bedroom to find Eva up, showered, boiling water and making toast. With her in it, my kitchen looked seedy. My rooms were like my head, better at night. Eva had packed her small suitcase. It stood zipped by the door. We talked. We watched the clock. Eva's car would arrive any minute. The weekend had gone by too fast. There was never enough time. I heard myself speak these endearments. The voice I used, the face I wore only for Eva. From my sister I hid the fact that I was depressed. On the cusp of graduating, I had no idea what my future would look like, I was in an in-between state, everything I did felt like moving against fast water. The weight of Eva's need, my responsibility for her happiness. Eva told me she missed me. I never came to the house anymore. I know, I said, and let my reply sound there like an off-note. I could not tell Eva that I wasn't tolerated, my love for her was a perseverant love, a seductive love, I wanted to wrest her from Cherry's control. I got up from the table, searched the kitchen cupboards. I offered Eva a bag of chips for the drive, but she said no, she'd be fine. I knew she would never swallow fat, but I pushed to see whether she was sure, it was a long trip. She was sure. I told my sister I was sorry I didn't have something better to give.

Don't be sorry for anything, Eva said. Last night was the best night of my life.

We are identical when I am drunk. I spoke in Eva's high, dutiful voice, the staccato of her hiccups. I asked whether that was how she really saw me.

Oh, that—she laughed at my impression and shrugged her shoulders. You're free, that's all, Eva said, I envy your freedom.

I pictured Margot Hemingway's gravestone. *Free spirit freed. Free* was code for reckless. Reckless spirit wrecked. I drank my coffee, wound my fingers through my sister's. Eva told me she did not have friends because she had no time for friendship. Her parents barely spoke and their silence was like a bomb only she could defuse. The pressure she felt was lethal. She could not make a misstep. Then Eva said, The second you're born your parents start to describe you back to yourself and you become that person. They keep telling me that you and I are exact opposites and I don't believe it. I hate seeing myself from the outside. It has this hall-of-mirrors effect. I can never get to my real self because of these endless reflections. Only with you am I real. And, I'm not even your sister. I'm your *half*-sister.

You are my sister, I replied. I refuse to make a fraction out of a relationship I feel is more than whole.

Eva's phone pinged. Her driver was here.

The town car idling beside us, Eva and I embraced until I pulled away to study my sister's clean, scrubbed face. She looked fresh off a win. She congratulated me again on my performance, searching for compliments instead of giving them. You were. You were. You were. I told Eva we were identical in the parts of ourselves that our parents could not see or even imagine and those were the parts that mattered. Then I thanked her for travelling all these miles just to watch some minor college show. Hardly, Eva said in just the way I did, dropping her pitch and spiking her tone. Eva got in the car. I stood on the sidewalk in my satin robe and waved until the black car disappeared from view.

I had lost Eva. I had lost Paul. At last, I made use of my free spirit and left the metal bench.

.   .   .

Cherry watched Mona cross the sculpture garden and noted a few other people turn their heads to track this injured-looking girl with their eyes. Mona's dress was backless, and Cherry could see Mona's shoulder blades starkly exposed, the hard beads of her spine. The dress was cut beneath her

tailbone and Cherry could make out the upper band of
Mona's black underwear. It was lace. As she walked, Mona
appeared to be reconstituting herself, adding substance to
bone. Her posture became angry and prideful as a swan's.
There was no parting look over the shoulder for Cherry.
Mona stopped in front of the Rodin bronze and began taking
photos of the sculpture with her phone. She took a selfie
with John the Baptist. Mona, shaped like a dagger, gazing
deadpan into her lens with John. Why him? Wasn't he just
another John convinced he had a private line to the higher
realm? Try being a Joan with a private line. You get burned
at the stake. Cherry wanted to laugh but couldn't because
it wasn't funny. Now Mona was texting. She was probably
sending the photo to her brooding boyfriend, Wes, or
maybe that sexy nun, Ani. Curled around her phone, she
was oblivious. Just then a gaudy woman entered the sculpture garden and obscured Cherry's view of Mona. The
woman was dressed like a brooch, an ornamental thing pin-
ning herself desperately to life. No one seemed to understand the height of fashion was when the effort to dress was
made invisible by the wearer. The gaudy woman found a
bench, and with her view restored, Cherry saw Mona was
gone. She felt empty. The remaining hours of the afternoon
stretched blank before her. Eva had moved out. Paul was in
his study. He said he was writing but who knows, the door
was closed. Must be nice to sit there all day believing your
thoughts could be sold. The problem was her love for Paul.

His star might be fading, but her love was incontrovertible. Cherry would walk the museum. She needed to be surrounded by art that was resolved enough to be framed. Cherry knew she could not touch the art, but she felt compelled by the prospect. But really, if she touched the art, would she be ejected from the building? A wing was named for her family. The ends of her fingers were clean.

Reapplying her lipstick, Cherry thought back to when Mona was first discovered and cast in that film. The story was that Mona was alone on a train platform. The director said it was nearly imperceptible, but he felt her sadness radiate through the underground of the city. From a distance, the director watched this stone-faced girl. He watched her pace the platform and then drive her fist into her jawbone. The girl ignored the passing trains. What Cherry would never know was that Mona, a self-described nobody, a student at an unexceptional high school, had ended up in the station after wandering the streets for hours, telling her mother she was at the library, she was studying, she would be late getting home, then buying a pregnancy test, going into a public washroom, squatting above the seat, peeing on the stick with her face slack, her eyes wet with dread, picturing then unpicturing her child, knowing what was to come.

.   .   .

On the train back to the apartment, I studied my blond reflection. The speeding train made my reflection a filmstrip. In flash cuts, I was Margot. I was Margaux. I was Margot. *Margot Hemingway became a supermodel overnight, and overnight she vanished—into alcohol, bad marriages, rivalry with sister Mariel and thoughts of suicide. At Betty Ford, she faced the truth. This is her story.* Paul's secret had been blown. His fate was no longer superimposed on mine. I would do my show and my show would revive me.

TWO

A year into the estrangement, I sent an email to Eva. Paul and Cherry had moved forward so I reasoned we should too. Eva and I still had not spoken, not since I got her letter. In the weeks following Paul's confession, I had called Eva. This was Ani's advice. Call Eva, remind her who you are, Eva does not see people as people, she sees them as ideas. I stopped my calls to Eva when I went into a month of rehearsals for *Margot*. Rehearsing, I was in a cocoon—Eva's letter, arriving just before my final dress rehearsal, disrupted my cocoon. I opened my show, ran the show, my show was extended. After an especially good performance, I would call Eva, my blood coursing with adrenaline, and leave her affectionate voice messages. My messages went unanswered.

After Paul's reconciliation with Cherry, Paul's world was closed to me. It was as if a seam had briefly, unnaturally opened, and I had been pulled through it. Now the seam was closed, I had been pushed back out, and once more, I was in the shadows of Paul's life. Paul and I spoke infrequently, and when we did, it was quick and surface-level, there was a feeling of polite disorientation between us, as if we did not know the rules of this new arrangement, but our closeness had obliterated the family so we had better play it safe. As our distance grew and became habitual, I felt less and less hurt by him, he became an abstraction to me. With Paul receded, my life returned. I toured my play, and felt re-ordered by the act of performance. Night after night, I followed a set of actions timed down to the second. Think of the precision of a lighting cue, a sound cue, an entrance, an exit. For a year, I knew exactly where to place my body, what to say. After the closing performance of *Margot*, I stepped off the stage, into Wes's arms, and I felt invincible. But when I returned to the apartment, with no outlet or structure for my energy, I was open and aimless again, it was Eva who entered then dominated my thoughts. I'd been commissioned to write my next play. I was supposed to be writing my next play. Instead, I wrote to Eva. I drafted emails to Eva. I laboured and obsessed over Eva. I chased Eva in my mind. Eventually, I edited my words down and hit send. In my email, I copied Juliet, Cherry and Paul. I also copied Cherry's sons who were now venture capitalists after receiving a big sum from Cherry's mother's estate. I wrote that we were all at pivotal points in our lives. Eva had transferred from philosophy into pre-med, Juliet had a beautiful new baby, I had finished touring my play. Why not try to find some resolution within the family? I apologized for the pain I had caused everyone, especially as it had impacted Eva.

The first response came from Paul, a couple of days later. Copying the group, he wrote that he, Eva and Cher were in Moscow. He was doing research for his next novel. He asked that we not raise the subject of his next novel, even obliquely. They had a guide who seemed to know everything about everything. The weather was good. Paul wrote that he had nothing to do with my proposal, but hoped it would receive the constructive response it deserved.

Then Juliet responded. She had a son now. She would position her phone so I could watch her son sleep. We joked there was something demented about our love, our love was surveillance, we were stalking her son. Then Juliet told me it was the other way around. Her son was stalking her. She had no psychological privacy. He was always there, she was never alone. The moment she'd watched him exit her body, her mind was divided. Time was slow, time was fast. She had never felt more like herself, less like herself. She said she knew that someday I would understand. But would I, I thought. I had always had the premonition that my body would not be able to make a life. I had confided this feeling once to Ani, not to Juliet, and never to Wes. I had been pregnant before and ended the pregnancy, so the fear had no logic, but it lingered there in the outskirts of my mind. I would talk myself out of it. It was a childish habit, sprung from hurt, another way of telling myself I was alone in the world. Surely, Wes and I would parent together. We were not the endpoint of our love. I saw the change in Juliet when she went from daughter to mother. The mortal tendon between her and her son. I wanted that. I wanted to be a mother.

In her email to the group, Juliet wrote that she and I were not evil people, despite how we had been characterized, especially over this last year, and that the family's current state was the result of a series of breaks in trust. Irreparable damage had been done. To pretend otherwise would be dishonest. Our family was at war, divided by blood, and while that war could be ended, and a truce declared, the divide was something we couldn't change. She wrote that, by the way, she now had a baby, and her baby was eight months old, and only Mona had recognized his birth, only Mona had flown over to meet him, and the pain that had caused her far surpassed whatever pain we were talking about here. She wrote that life was short, and if Cherry and Cherry's sons and Eva wanted to keep fighting with us, that was too bad, she was out of energy. Then she wrote that the current state was everyone's doing, and she had optimism that with small steps we might one day see each other for who we really are. Then she wrote: I would love a reaction.

Eva reacted. Eva wrote that whoever Juliet's baby was, whatever her/his name might be, her/his birthweight and star sign, she/he did not even know that Eva existed, so how could Eva have caused her/him any pain, whereas Eva's own sisters, sisters whom she had trusted, had betrayed her over a prolonged period of time. Eva wrote that at least I had tried to reach out to her, but in a year, Juliet had not. Then Eva thought back on her life, and how Juliet was hardly in it. Eva had no memories of Juliet, no feeling of closeness with Juliet other than what her title, *half-sister*, implied. Juliet was, in a word, inconsequential to the matter of Eva's life. When Eva hit her lowest point, after learning of Paul's affair, my part in abetting it, and the risk it presented to her parents' marriage, Juliet's absence was fitting. Eva then repeated what she had written to me about being good and trustworthy, and that Juliet did not meet Eva's conditions for a relationship. Juliet had acted immorally. She was obviously still held back by her past issues, specifically, Paul leaving us for Cherry and our mother's failed suicide attempt. Juliet was emotionally and intellectually arrested. She had a long way to go as a person. Then Eva told Juliet that if she worked toward meeting Eva's criteria, there was a chance Eva might let her back into her life, but this was unlikely given their record and Juliet's shortcomings.

Juliet wrote to Eva to say thank you very much for your diagnosis, Eva. She was sorry her actions continued to disappoint, she was doing her best which would clearly never satisfy Eva's standards. She was sorry to be perceived as immoral and arrested, and it would seem her attempt to move the conversation forward had only backfired and caused more pain. Good luck with your life, she wrote to Eva, and thank you again for your expertise on mine. Enjoy Moscow.

Then Juliet wrote to Paul. She copied me. Eva was sixteen years younger than Juliet. Who made her God? Were they passing the keyboard between them at their five-star hotel? How could Paul stand it? And where was Cherry in this? Once again, watching it all burn.

Eva then wrote to Juliet to say it was she who should be wishing Juliet good luck with her life. I don't need luck, Eva wrote.

Paul intercepted. Copying me, Paul wrote to Juliet asking that she please not respond to Eva until he had had some time to think it through. He was still in Moscow with Cher and Eva, on to Helsinki the following day.

Juliet replied to Paul that his request made sense, she would not respond to Eva, she had her dignity. She refused to be treated like a thoughtless pig. He and Cherry had raised a very disturbed girl. Eva hated Juliet and she hated me, and we were not put in this world to be hated.

Cherry's eldest son wrote to Juliet to say that Juliet's war analogy was a weak projection as the only war was the one being fought inside Juliet. Juliet needed crisper goals. Eva had prescribed a way forward, and now it was up to me and Juliet to prove ourselves. Were we good? Were we trustworthy? Were we qualifiers? TBD. He didn't know, but Eva would. Then he wrote to Juliet, I am not a father yet, but I have no stronger motivation than my future child. You need to do better by Eva, Juliet. And you need to do better by your son.

Juliet wrote to Paul. Who were these assholes? The fact that she and I were being held to terms like *goodness* and *trust* was fucked up, and Paul knew it. She had a really hard time being committed to a set of conditions in order to rejoin a family that had never treated us like family in the first place. She refused to be portrayed as a bad person. This mess was the result of a broken relationship between Paul and Cherry, and how convenient that right in front of their eyes, she and I were taking the fall while they came out blameless. Did Paul not see how much I had debased myself to get this whole effort going in the first place? You would think Mona had had the affair, Juliet wrote. Why is she the one apologizing? Then Juliet wrote, Oh, and by the way, if you or Cherry were planning to intervene, it is too late now. No one is going to listen to anyone but Eva.

Paul responded that he was still travelling. He and Cher and Eva were in Helsinki now. It was a perfectly decent day, but the birds outside his hotel window did not fly like the birds in Moscow, they flew without conviction, without real intent. He would try to call. He was sorry this was so upsetting for Juliet.

—

I wrote to Juliet, Only in the company of Cherry and Eva would Paul find fault in birds.

It's an allegory, Juliet shot back. We're the sulking birds.

Then I wrote to Paul. I told him to call Juliet, and to make time for a long conversation. She was isolated and in a bad way.

After I sent the email to Paul, I tried to ignore the creep of contentment I felt. After a void of a year, through which we had held each other at a distance, discussed only what was in front of us and never what was inside, I had the chance to reconnect with my father.

Paul sent an email to Juliet. He copied me. He was worn out. He was filled with self-loathing. Writing love scenes in the Red Square. He had become a caricature of himself. His writing was inert. His every sentence dead. He could not take on Juliet's despair. Paul wrote that he loved Juliet, she was his daughter, and for what it was worth, Cherry felt the same way. He wrote that life did not always come together in the way we wanted it to, and that the most troubling aspect of this whole exchange had been Juliet's anger. Paul wrote that Juliet's anger originated with his separation from Natasha. Paul asked that Juliet stop denigrating Cherry, Cherry's sons and Eva. Cherry had always been supportive of Juliet and me. She had worked tirelessly to consolidate the family.

She had given up so much in the service of Paul's writing. Without Cherry, he would probably be teaching night school. Paul wrote that while he and Cherry wanted the family to function, the children were adults now, and he and Cherry were in no position to dictate the way forward. The way forward was ours to determine. Paul suggested that Juliet stay out of the email exchange for now, but that I keep working away at it. Eva was fragile.

Juliet replied to Paul. To clarify, her anger did not originate with his separation from Natasha. That was a deeply flawed line Cherry had been feeding Paul for twenty years, and it would appear he was now officially brainwashed. Natasha had no bearing on her anger. Juliet's anger sat squarely with Cherry and Paul. When Paul moved in with Cherry, Cherry had presented Paul with an ultimatum. She said, It's me or your girls. When Paul and Cherry were renovating their big house, Cherry had eliminated our bedroom from the blueprint. We knew these things because Paul had told them to us. Paul stood by in Spain when Cherry screamed at me and sprayed me with a garden hose like an unwanted animal. Paul stood by when Cherry, after I'd gotten my period for the first time, offered me a diaper. Paul stood by more times than Juliet was willing to count, she didn't have the intestinal fortitude to count. Paul should be the one counting. Paul raised Cherry's sons and Paul raised Eva. Paul travelled the world with them, he said goodnight to them. They had a ski chalet Juliet and I were prohibited from using so it stood empty in the off-season out of spite. In sum, she had seen no evidence of Cherry consolidating the family. Meanwhile, Paul told us that we were his true loves. Paul confided in us and we protected him. Paul had broken a confidence with me. Cherry then broke a confidence with Paul. That was why their children were no longer speaking to each other. While she would never understand the self-satisfied monster Eva had become, it was better for Eva to have Juliet and me be scapegoats for her misery rather than her parents. It was critical to Eva's stability in her life and satisfaction in her life that she have parents she could love and trust, and Juliet would just leave it at that. Then Juliet wrote that whenever her baby appeared angry, it was because he was hungry or tired. She wrote that she was not all that different from her baby.

Paul never responded to Juliet's email, or the group exchange, but he started to get in touch with me. He would forward, he wrote, for my own interest and entertainment, Eva's emails detailing her adventures abroad. Eva was doing a clinical research internship at a mental health institute in Malmö, she was in Mozambique diving off the north shore, she was hiking glaciers on the western peninsula of Iceland. Eva had decided to be a psychiatrist. She was continuing with her pre-med studies in the fall on a full varsity rowing scholarship. Paul was proud and relieved, Eva seemed to have found some equanimity.

Go Eva, I wrote to Paul.

.   .   .

Midsummer, Paul invited Wes and me up to the new island home. Paul said the invitation was Cherry's idea. The bulk of the construction had been completed, they were keen for us to see it. The house had just been featured in an architecture magazine, and Paul said float planes buzzed overhead day and night trying to get a closer look. Cherry wrote that she hoped we would have many happy times there. Wes said, We'd better draft our wills. They told us the place was still pretty bare, they had hardly moved anything in, so to bring a tent and sleeping bags. They also needed milk for their coffee. We said okay and then tried to guess at the motives behind their invitation, but could not. Ultimately, we were more curious than hesitant, we wanted to see the island home, it symbolized the resurrection of Paul and Cherry's relationship, and though we left this desire unexpressed, I knew both Wes and I wanted time with Paul. He was my father, and in a refractory way, he was Wes's now too. We parked at the marina and took a water taxi to the island, which was about a thirty-minute drive into open water. It was very rough, and a couple of times, Wes and I felt we might be thrown from the boat. Wes was nervous, he was not a strong swimmer. He had never been in a motorboat before, he knew the story of Cherry's father's death. When we arrived, Wes gave Paul a bottle of wine, and Paul commented that the wine was a young wine, and Wes said he didn't know if that was a good thing or a bad thing, and Paul laughed and touched Wes's shoulder like an anointment. Cherry said we looked as though we'd just come from a nightclub. Then she blinked like a machine and said, Welcome. Cherry and Paul walked us around the island, the island was huge and sprawling, I don't know what I had pictured, but it was not this. The island was an outcropping of rock surrounded by massive water, with inlets and forested areas, and an entire section covered in poison ivy that we observed from a distance, with outlying slabs of granite you could swim to or walk to depending on the water level. It was very remote, and Cherry and Paul seemed proud of this fact. The shoreline was made up of stacked boulders and Cherry told us they planned to have the boulders removed and sand brought in. Cherry would hire someone to sculpt the sand into dunes. Wes asked if the boulders didn't serve a purpose by forming a barrier against hurricanes and high seas. Cherry replied that sand was rock, rock was sand, and a beach would make it easier to enter the water and everybody wanted that. They indicated the best spots to swim, where a deer had washed up on the shore earlier in the season, where the helipad would go, where the sleeping cabins were going to be built, and Paul's writing studio. Wes and I knew better than to ask after Paul's work. Paul had not published since *Daughter*, it had been over fifteen years. We knew he had at least three finished manuscripts, but no one had read them other than Cherry. A mink scampered across the rock. Birds darted. We saw the framing had been put up for the boat-house. Paul and Cherry had just bought a large motorboat, it had twin engines, they told us, they needed something fail-safe to make the long trip out. They showed us the boat, it was deep green with white trim, and they had called it *Evangeline*. Wes said he needed to get out of the direct sun, he was allergic to the sun, and he could feel his skin starting to itch. Paul and Cherry led us up to the main house, a glass square, where we had a drink and dipped radishes in coarse salt. Cherry arranged stalks of flowers in a vase. She was the most alone of people. Night fell. Antiseptic stars. On a fold of newspaper, Cherry gutted a fish, then at the counter, cut parsley, lemon. She set out four plates, the silver. Paul pan-fried the fish. His hair stood windswept on end. He had his sunglasses perched on his forehead, wore the same white shirt and white trousers he had worn in Spain, threadbare and stained now, rolled at the cuffs. I'd forgotten how Paul cooked. It was stressful to watch. Cherry watched. Wes and I offered to help, we were waved away. When we had dinner, the four of us sat cross-legged on the floor and ate off our laps. There was no table yet, no chairs. Paul lit a fire in the fireplace. He wiped his brow. Things, Paul said, were coming together bit by bit. Cher was running the show, Paul said, and he put his hand on the back of her neck and let it rest there.

All around us, on the open water, we could see naval lights blinking red and green to keep boaters inside their proper channels. The sea, Cherry and Paul explained, was full of shoals. They pointed in the direction of a shipwreck, quite recent, an inexperienced sailor. There was a lighthouse within view and throughout dinner, its light swept around and around the room. We were cleaning up when Cherry said, Mona, what's your purpose? You cannot have a strategy, Cherry said, without a purpose. Then she said, Don't look so worried. She explained her question was part of a dinner party game she and Paul liked to play. She said it forced you to state your strategy, and then she repeated, You cannot have a strategy without a purpose. That doesn't sound like much of a game, I said. And Cherry smiled and said in a confiding tone, I'm trying to help you. You seem lost so much of the time. Then she asked me how the theatre business was going, what plays she should see, who was up and coming, and I told Cherry I was doing mostly film work now. I was writing the sequel to *Margot* but it was slow going, and the film work was holding my attention. Oh? said Cherry. I am currently playing a woman, I answered, mourning her father in a hostile landscape. Cherry said, It must be boring

to play the victim over and over. I don't see it that way, I—.
Cherry cut me off. You know, Cherry said, her reptile eyes
eager and darkening, You were such a sombre girl, a real sob
story. Paul and I used to call you Tragedia. Whenever Paul
mentioned your name, we would make rain with our hands.
Tragedia. Then Cherry touched the thin gold chain at her
neck and asked, How long do you think it takes to swim
around this island? I have no idea, I stammered too loudly,
my voice out of control, An hour? Two?

Eva did it in seventeen minutes.

In a different corner of the glass room, I could hear Paul
talking to Wes about his art projects. He asked Wes how he
planned to make any money. Wes told Paul that he was actually opening an art gallery, his own gallery, and Paul said,
Wouldn't that be even less financially secure than making
and selling your own art? When you're a gallerist, Paul said,
you're responsible for other people's failures. When you're
an artist, you're only responsible for your own. I guess that's
true, Wes said, but told Paul that he was doing it anyway.
Paul said, You'll probably have a hard time getting investors.
We'll see, Wes said. Paul said, You wouldn't have had a hard
time getting investors if you'd stayed in the acting game,
you could've been the next what's-his-name, you know, that
guy. Wes said, I guess I value my soul. Well don't, Paul said,
it will only get you in trouble. Then Wes asked Paul how
the novel was coming, and Paul said he couldn't talk about

it, it was like letting light into the darkroom, and he didn't want to spoil the film. I had heard Paul use this analogy. Wes had too, and he said so to Paul. Wes hung there inside the silence between them until Paul moved away. Then Wes left that corner of the glass room, and came to stand with me. Cherry and Paul had leaned the Rothko against one of the glass walls. Cherry asked Wes what he thought of the painting. Restraint or limitation? Restraint, Wes answered, sounding aghast. Then Cherry turned to me. Do you like the painting, Mona? I love it, I answered. I wouldn't trust anyone who didn't. And then Wes asked about the shotgun lying near the painting, and Paul said it was for the geese, they're a fucking nuisance, they shit everywhere, they have no song, they're stupid fucking birds.

Wes and I were leaving the following morning when a barge crept past us toward Paul and Cherry's island. Speeding by in the water taxi, we could see, on the back of the barge, wrapped in clear plastic, a white sectional couch. Cherry had had it imported from France. She had told us about the couch the night before over dinner, and when Wes had asked how a couch travels from France, Cherry joked, first-class. Then she asked Wes what Wes was short for, and Wes said, Nothing.

When Wes and I got back to the city, I told him I felt like I was betraying Juliet by socializing with Cherry. Wes said,

That did not feel social. We drove longer than we stayed. We spent a hundred dollars on gas. Wes said he felt spun. He lay on the floor. After a pause, Wes said, What does evil think it is? I mean who is she to herself? And sand is not rock, Cherry. Sand is the end of rock. I wouldn't be inexact with the ocean. Wes rolled onto his side. He stretched out. Wearily, he said, Maybe getting on with people is never a bad thing. But is that true? I asked Wes, and he said in this case, he didn't know, it was so hard to tell what was real and what was not, Like is your father a captive or a mastermind?

.   .   .

A month passed and Paul called to tell me Eva was in the city. She is pretty shattered, Paul said. Pre-med. Then he suggested I reach out to her. She would be here for a few days. I told Paul I had a lot going on. We all do, Paul responded. Then he sucked in his breath, he must have been smoking, and he said, Please, Mona. I thought back to the island visit. Paul had been agitated, melodramatic, drank heavily, told Wes he was the son he always wanted, then was in a rush to see us go, practically pushed us into the water taxi. Paul mostly ignored me. Had Cherry asked about my work to spite Paul? I didn't know. I could not track the various ways they hurt each other. On the phone with Paul, I told him I had five minutes to talk, I was on set. He could probably hear the airplanes overhead. The director and I

were in a landscape near the airport, it was like the bad-
lands, and the director, well—The director just watches
me through his lens, I told Paul. There is no script. The
only plot point is that my father has just died. Huh, Paul
said, I'd better take cover. The director might be filming
me right now, I told Paul, he might be filming this call. The
film was like that. The director just filmed me peeing. Jesus,
Paul said. Are you getting paid? Don't answer that. Then
Paul told me he could not go on with the situation as it was.
We had to find a way to reconcile. Our reconciliation would
relieve him of his despair. His despair was spilling over into
everything. Paul said he would turn seventy next spring
and he wanted his daughters around him. If we weren't
around him, we should just put him in the ground. His
blood pressure had gone up. He'd been strong-armed by
Cherry into taking anti-anxiety meds. The meds blunted
the edges of the world, the edges of himself. Language had
no hold over him. He could not write one true sentence. He
was like the fucking geese, honking impotently through
the night. *Chekhov! Tolstoy! Nabokov!* Paul imitated the geese.
He needed to get off the medication. He needed to publish
again. Either the world was waiting for him or the world
had forgotten him, both scenarios depressed him horribly.
I interrupted Paul to ask him where he was, he sounded
breathless, like he was being chased. I asked Paul if he was
being chased by Cherry. Very funny, Paul said, and then he
told me he was walking the stone path down to the pond.

He said he needed to look at the water. He was at the water now. He could see men fishing the opposite shore. I used to be one of those men, Paul said. Then Paul said our estrangement needed to end. If I looked back on my life, I would see that he had done enough nice things for me to make a request like this one in turn. Haven't I? Paul said. Aren't you going to say something? Say something, Mona. I'm pregnant, I told Paul. In the receiver, I heard Paul's breath change. Are you still there? I asked Paul. And in a strangled voice, Paul answered, Remember this feeling. It is the only one that counts.

That night, I wrote to Eva from bed. My skin was still hot to the touch from being in the sun all day. The director had me in a sheer dress and running shoes. He trained his lens on the ants in the dirt and then he trained his lens on me. There was a coating of dirt on my skin, the residue of tears on my face. I could taste the salt and dirt in my mouth, my skin was browned from the sun, my hair matted and dry. There was no shade. I was too tired to bathe. I felt spent, hollowed out. I had cried that afternoon. After speaking with Paul. The director filmed me for a long time, said *Cut* and then thanked me. For what, I asked the director, crying? Yeah, the director answered. Any time, I said.

Taking a winding route home, the director drove me back to the apartment, shaking me awake once we'd reached the building. I climbed the stairs thinking of what I would tell Wes. Crying is the face's nude scene. That was what I would tell Wes. He would like that. Wes was in the kitchen making dinner. He was shirtless, in work trousers held up with a shoelace, his hazmat suit hanging from a peg by the door. I kissed Wes's shoulder, his mouth. He had a trapped look on his face which I did not want to see. He was focused on making dinner and he communicated this to me with his hard, ropy body, the severity of his gestures. Wes did not want to hear about the shoot. I thought of the call with Paul, telling Paul our news. I brought the dissonance to the relationship with Wes. I withdrew, went into the bedroom. Through the wall, I could hear Wes clanging metal as if he were issuing some kind of bitter code. Look at who you are, Mona, look at who you've made me. I lay down on the bed. Once I'd shifted my body, I saw the mental pattern at work. I was fast-forwarding to our end, to the night Wes would leave me, convinced my life would be my mother's. Wes was probably just hungry. I kept my distance from Wes, put on my headphones.

I emailed Eva. I proposed we meet before she returned to school. I told her that Cherry and I were fixing things between us. This was obviously a lie. The island visit had been full of mind games. Eva had written to me about being *good* and *trustworthy*. Did one not cover the other? I guessed not. I guessed a person could be both good and untrustworthy. I apologized again for the hurt I had caused her. I recognized that she had suffered a betrayal, and I took responsibility for my part in that betrayal. Then, I gave Eva an update. I told her about the film. I told her I still picked up shifts at the bar. Wes was just as she remembered. He was doing his art installations. He had totally forsaken acting, which no one understood, but Wes was not interested in being understood. He was planning on opening a gallery. He and some other artist friends had been working on the gallery space, preparing it for opening, and found they needed a place to sit. Wes pulled a couch in off the curb, and the gallery was infested with bedbugs. Once the fumigation guys left, Wes saw that he could make a lot more money as an exterminator, so he was working in fumigation now. It was going well, really well, actually. There was always someone who had something living in their house they did not want there. I went on. I told Eva we were married earlier that summer at City Hall with Ani and Wes's best friend, Jason, in attendance. Afterward we went to a fancy hotel for champagne. We got very drunk. Soon after, I found out I was pregnant. I was not far along, only a couple of months, but I was writing because I wanted Eva to be part of our child's life. In my email I described to Eva what being pregnant was like, but then I deleted my description. I felt protective of my pregnancy in Eva's presence, even imagined. Then I nearly deleted the entire email to Eva. What was I doing? Who was I pursuing? I did not tell Eva that Wes and I had eloped because it was the only way. We could not combine Paul with

Natasha with Cherry with Juliet, who would have to fly overseas with her young son. And by eloping, I shielded myself from Eva. Eva would have ignored my invitation. It was not that I was dead to Eva, I was subhuman, and Eva would take the opportunity of my wedding day to reinforce this fact. And more, I could not face the prospect of Paul playing father to the bride. Getting drunk and, in his seductive way, overshadowing the event. Wait. I closed my eyes. What kind of speech would Paul have made for me? Had I missed my one chance to hear what Paul thought of me, how Paul saw me, who I was to Paul? I called for Wes and he brought me a box of saltines, a glass of water. He asked me what I was doing. I said I was writing to Eva. Why bother? Wes asked. She is in the city, I answered. But Eva has ceased being Eva, Wes said and he left the bedroom. When Wes and I told Paul and Cherry we'd eloped, they sent flowers to the apartment. The bouquet was ugly, a clash of raw emotion, more suited to a funeral. I knew Paul had arranged for the flowers. I dried the bouquet and nailed it to the wall in our living room, loosening plaster dust. I felt lightheaded and sat down, the hammer still in my hand. Was Paul stung that he did not get to walk me down the aisle, that I had eliminated his role? Maybe as Paul hurt me, I hurt Paul. In bed, I lay my hands on my stomach. Beside me, my laptop was still open. The screen went black. We had listened to the baby's heartbeat the week before and it sounded like a distress signal. Oh no, I said to the technician, and the technician said, no worries, that's how they always sound, fast and loud. When Juliet became a mother, she got closer to the truth of life as she perceived it. Here I was hurtling farther into the past. I decided to finish my email to Eva. It would be my last attempt to reach her.

Eva did not respond. More than a year and a half had passed since Eva sent her letter cutting off contact. Eva would stand her ground even if her position was outdated. She finally had control over Paul. She had Paul's desperate attention, and this felt close enough to love. What mattered to Eva was supremacy. Did I mean what I had written to Eva? Did I want to meet with Eva, fix things between us and move forward? I had blind-copied Paul on the email. It struck me then that I had written to Eva not to recover a relationship with Eva, but to recover one with Paul. Paul was the one I wanted to see. Paul was the one I wanted in my child's life.

.   .   .

It was early December. The sky was steel grey and exerted a cold pressure. It was a brutalist sky. No snow yet. We were sitting in Paul's favourite restaurant. The server was going from table to table flicking his lighter, lighting the candle at the centre of each table, making the room very pretty. It was night. The sinking, bottomless hours of winter. Our plates had been cleared when I told Paul that I knew I was pregnant the moment I smelled the glue binding the slats of wood in our apartment. That must be a predator-prey thing, Paul said, looking down at the small, hard curve of my stomach. Like your body has to be alert to new dangers or something. That makes sense, I responded to Paul. My father's eyes were dull, his movements heavy and slurred. I felt like a conductor and he could speak only on my cue. I had never seen Paul this way, the vitality and colour seeped from him. He was like a photocopy of a photocopy of himself. I told Paul I would help him get off the anti-anxiety meds. He scoffed, reached for his wine. I told him that the world had not forgotten him, the world was waiting. Stop, Mona. Paul slashed the air with his hand. It was too defeating to talk about his writing. His writing allowed him to gain altitude, and now, in this slump or implosion or death spiral or whatever you wanted to call it, the opposite was true. He was buried alive. Paul drank his wine. He motioned for the server, ordered more. The restaurant was not busy. My state is pitiful, Paul muttered. Let's change the subject. He rubbed his hands and said, So. Paul asked me how my work was going, what I was thinking about these days, where I wanted to take my next play. I told Paul I was nearly finished with the sequel to *Margot*. It had been a slog. Writing a follow-up was so intimidating. Paul nodded, folded his arms defensively. I told Paul I was lecturing at a literary festival, I was headed there next week. The lecture was about the hazards of biographical theatre, about what art can and cannot do, what life is and is not—Paul did a fake yawn. We laughed. Then Paul did a real yawn. He shook his head and apologized for being bad company. The meds, he said, he was bludgeoned by the meds. Sounds like things are going well, Paul said, inflating his tone with false sentiment. Then Paul reached across the table and pulled me to him. Never write a novel, Mona. You'd find it tedious. There's so much description. Unlike me, you chase life. Theatre is closer to life. Theatre is talking. Well actually, I said to Paul, releasing myself from his grip, theatre is a lot more than talking. That's pretty reductive. I mean a novel is a lot more than description, don't you think? I don't know, Paul said, I used to believe in the shape of words. He trailed off, took in the flickering room. And then speaking to the room, Paul said, I cursed myself. When I left your mother, I left behind my gift. The comment was strange and it repelled me. Give me a minute, I told Paul, retrieving my phone from my dress pocket. Wes is close by, I explained to my father, and he wants to walk me home. *Deus ex machina*, I texted Wes. Forget what I said about Natasha, Paul was saying now, gregariously, remaking the atmosphere between us. She's sensational, like you, that's all. Then Paul laughed and he morphed into a second Paul. He was now the outward-facing Paul, his skin flushed pink with the wine, his self a black hole. My father's eyes turned an unnatural green, they were like liquid detergent, and as I sat across from my father in his favourite restaurant, they shone for me. Look at you, Paul said. Then he asked me how the pregnancy was going.

I told Paul I had entered my second trimester. I wished I could give him some of my energy. I'm a fucking dynamo, I told Paul. I have twice my blood volume. I'm growing eyeballs and fingernails and vital organs. Wes was building a crib for the baby. We didn't know if the baby was a girl or a boy, we didn't want to know. I could hear the excitement in my voice. I looked down at this body I was describing. I put my hands on my stomach and felt my child roll and turn beneath them like sea life. We were in contact. The complete union. Then Wes was at the table, the shoulders of his parka dusted with snow. There was snow in Wes's dark hair. It looked like confetti and I told him so. Wes touched my stomach, kissed my mouth, held my face and looked into me. Paul pushed his chair back. He stood, gripping the edge of the table for balance, and then he embraced Wes. He clapped Wes on the back, and said, Son. Paul asked Wes if he wanted a drink, something to eat, did he want anything at all, the kitchen was still open. Paul was angling for us to stay. Wes glanced over to me. I telegraphed *No* with my eyes. Wes told Paul another time, we needed to go. I kissed my father's cheek, and patting his arm, thanked him for the meal, but he was already elsewhere in his mind, on to the next thing. I got my coat from the coat check and glanced back at my father, alone in the romantic room. The server congratulated me. He stood behind me and helped me into my coat. I laced my arms through the sleeves and the server adjusted the coat to rest on my shoulders. Walking home, Wes asked about the dinner. I recounted the conversation with Paul. Wes felt that Paul was staking his claim to fiction. Paul was saying he was the novelist and I was the playwright. Maybe, I said to Wes. I described Paul, how he went abruptly from state to state. The bizarre words about Natasha. Wes nodded, he could see what I meant, Paul seemed deflated. We walked. The snow decorated us. I told Wes I had never felt happier. Same, Wes said. I told Wes I felt so lucky. I felt my luck was dangerous, like I should just go into hiding until the baby comes. Let's go into hiding, Wes said. I would be so into that. A long and easy silence.

. . .

I was on a flight home when I started to bleed. Wes picked me up from the airport, and we called our midwife who ordered an ultrasound. She said she couldn't promise anything. I was four and a half months pregnant, twenty-two weeks. After the ultrasound, Wes and I were sitting in a small room in an office tower downtown. Across from us, there were two sympathetic faces. They were telling us the baby was gone. He had died in utero, and they were very sorry. They could only get me in to the hospital for the following morning, we should plan to be there for at least one night. The pregnancy was too far along for surgery. I would have to labour. In the hospital room the following morning, I was given two pills. The doctor said he was very sorry when he gave me the pills.

I lay in the hospital bed. I had an IV. There was a button I could press that would make a painkiller go into my body. I kept pressing it. The labour was taking a long time. A doctor came in and he did a pelvic exam, and I told the nurse that the doctor touched me as if he hated me, he was not to come back, I didn't ever want to see his face again. By now, it was night, the labour was taking a long time. It was December, Wes was beside me. The baby came, and he was dead, and they put him on my chest. I kept him there all night. No one other than Wes was to touch him. A nurse came in and asked whether I wanted to see the chaplain and I said no. The two sympathetic faces, the ones from the small room in the office tower, came in just before the sun came up, they said they were there to support me and Wes and to meet the baby and that the baby was beautiful, he looked just like us. The nurses then came in and they explained that volunteers knit things for the babies in this ward, and we dressed the baby in a little crocheted suit and hat, and we took photos of him. Then they told me that it was time, he was beginning to turn, to change, they said, it was time, and they took him away.

.   .   .

Wes drove us home.

.   .   .

I called Ani. I told her that I didn't know where my baby was. At the hospital, we had made the arrangements, the baby would be cremated. We were given a pamphlet and Wes chose the funeral home. He said, Let's choose one that isn't close to us, one that we won't have to go by all the time. I told Ani I didn't know where my baby was. I didn't know if he was at the hospital still, if he was in the morgue there or if he was at the funeral home, I didn't know where my baby was. Ani hung up and then she called me back and said, He's at the funeral home, my girl, and tomorrow, you can pick up his ashes. And then she said, You don't have to say anything, but just stay on the phone.

. . .

Wes and I met at theatre school. I lived with Ani then, Ani was in the design department and Wes and I were both in the acting department. One night, Ani came home, it was a Sunday, and we were opening our final show, *Hamlet*, that Friday. Wes was playing Hamlet, I was playing Ophelia. We were a week away from graduating from our three-year program. That night, I was tired, I'd fought with the director. The director was called Sonny and he was sitting in the back row of the theatre checking sightlines when I erupted. I told Sonny that he wanted me to play Ophelia as an innocent, when really she was Joan of Arc. "She's not a girl who misses much"—I sang the line from "Happiness is a Warm

Gun"—and then I told Sonny that Ophelia went mad because she needed her love for Hamlet and her life to be like identical slides, one had to match the other when they overlapped, she couldn't live a lie. Sonny wanted Ophelia's mad scene to be sexy. He wanted her to have a hot death. He was staging her suicide like a Christian music video. He wanted to make a gift of her anguish because there was nothing more threatening than a woman who knows her own mind, then decides to die by it. Sonny said, Yeah, okay, thank you, Mona, and he got out of his seat and walked the aisle toward me, centre stage, and said, I did not kill Ophelia, Shakespeare killed Ophelia. We were shouting. The cast and crew cleared the theatre. I left hastily, forgetting to take off my costume. I was in my white nightdress and crown of flowers when Ani came through the front door of our apartment. It was around midnight. From my bedroom, I could hear her drop her bag, and with her back to the closed door, slide to the floor. She was sobbing.

Ani told me that Wes had broken up with her. He had been so withdrawn these last few weeks, but she thought it was the play, she didn't want to interfere, there was no larger role than Hamlet. Wes asked Ani if they could meet that night after the dress rehearsal. This was after your blowout with Sonny, Ani said. She was surprised that Wes wanted to meet, but reasoned that the following day was our dark day, he must have felt less pressure knowing we had the day off.

She told Wes sure, she had a few things to finish up. Ani was doing the set and costume design for the show so Wes understood. He said, of course, he would wait for her out front, he needed to get some air anyway. Ani felt excited to see Wes. They kissed outside the theatre. They held hands and decided to get takeout. They were mostly silent which was weird, but again, Ani felt he must be preoccupied, she didn't read into it. They got McDonald's and ate as they walked. Wes made a few remarks, not quite jokes, but almost jokes. You know, Ani said, how he does that blinking thing with his eyes when he is about to say something funny. He seemed nervous. He steered me to a park bench, and pulled his hand from mine. I knew the end was there before he said it. He told me he was in love with someone else and he hated himself for lying to me. Ani sobbed. I wrapped my arms around her. You're holding me too tight, Ani said, you're hurting me, her voice was louder now, and she pulled away. Ani said that she asked Wes who it was, and Wes replied that it didn't matter. He could never be with her anyway.

I dressed Ani for bed. I tucked her in, and stroked her hair, I sang the Marineland theme song. Ani laughed at that. I talked like Dennis Hopper from *Blue Velvet*. I inhaled sharply and reminded Ani that she had told me she had no interest in boyfriends, she didn't want a conventional life, sex was different, but finding sex was like finding air. Ani laughed and through her laughter said, Stop it, Mona, you're killing me. After a while, in the dark, Ani said I had been so hound-like in my listening about the break-up with Wes, she had revealed too much. With me, she was terrible with her secrets. I was too eager. Ani said everyone at the school treated pain as if it were some portal to insight. She told me she could train her mind. She had been a champion swimmer, she could focus her head, allow in only what was useful to her. She was a carpenter. She was precise. I never want to talk about this night again, Ani said. Promise, she said. I promise. I curled my body around Ani's, drifted, startled, then drifted, then woke in the cold sunlight. Ani was gone.

There were times in my friendship with Ani when I felt she was parasitic. I felt that the balance of giving was off, and I withdrew from Ani. The feeling would last for a few months, and it would weaken me like a low-level illness. It was like having the flu. Being without Ani was like being without my health. I would meet with Paul, and Paul would only cement my view that I was drawn to parasitic people, I punished myself by giving everything away, I was determined to leave myself worthless and empty. When I behaved this way, like a walled city, Ani let me be. She didn't question me. She saw it for what it was, a fit of self-protection. Ani was private, that was all. Ani had a base contentment. She was not porous and desperate for connection and approval like I was. She didn't want to read my mind the way I wanted to read hers.

She kept everything in. She was self-contained and vital. Ani was like her animated rooms.

I was the parasitic one.

Lying in Ani's bed, I thought about Wes. When Wes entered a room, I felt like I had been set on fire. I pretended the opposite, concentrating intensely on whatever it was that I was doing, getting a book from the library, stirring five packets of sugar into my coffee. That's a lot of sugar. Wes, towering beside me. Standing at the counter in the cafeteria with hardly any space between our bodies. The heat rushing to my face. The tight flip of my stomach. I said, you know Hamlet spelled backwards is Tell Ma? There, you've broken the code of the play, Mona, Wes said. You should be playing Hamlet. I'm serious, Mona. I'm serious. And I would walk away from him as quickly as I could. Even when Ani mentioned Wes, I looked down.

To the left of Ani's mirror was Ani's portrait of us. She had painted it earlier that year, in the fall. She had done the portrait from a photo taken the night we'd had the party, the night I was raped. I don't know who took the photo, I don't remember it being taken, it was taken from above. In the portrait, Ani and I are lying together on our couch. Ani is smoking. She is looking up at the ceiling, I have my head turned toward Ani, I am studying her face. From Ani's bed, looking at the portrait, I thought, That is the portrait of a good person and a bad person, and I am the bad person.

The night of the party, Ani and I decided to have a last-minute gathering in our apartment. It was a Sunday night, tomorrow would be our day off. Most of the acting and design departments arrived in waves. They climbed the three flights to our apartment, we could hear their voices in the narrow stairwell, they handed Ani and me bottles of wine from the corner store, embraced us and crowded into our apartment. Candles burned throughout the rooms. The windows fogged. Ani and I wore matching nurses' uniforms. I remember doing my lipstick in the dead screen of our television. Wes arrived late and did not stay long. He and Ani weren't together yet. I was in the kitchen, sitting on the counter and talking with the guest director, Magnus. Already, he had the nimbus of fame around him. Ani told me she'd heard Magnus was royalty somehow, fallen or former, she couldn't remember, there were still so many monarchies. Aside from that, she found him totally unremarkable. He is like a piece of bread, Ani said. With Magnus, we were doing *Medea*. We had been working with him for three weeks. We would open in another three. The party marked our midpoint. The process had been hard on us. A few of the actors, Wes among them, felt Magnus was a sadist. Magnus practiced what he called the theatre of sacrifice. On our first day, Magnus said,

Here are the rules for the next six weeks, no looking in the mirror, no washing hair, only candles after sunset, no meat, no sugar, only food you have cooked yourself, no swearing, no masturbation, no sex. There were eight of us in the cast. We were each given an elastic band to wear around our wrist. If we broke a rule, we snapped the elastic. Magnus demonstrated on Wes. Laughing, he pulled the elastic back on Wes's wrist, and said with it stretched taut, What's with you, Wes? With your Jesus hair. I bet you play the cello. Okay, he actually does, one of my classmates said. You're like a fucking centaur or something, Magnus went on, everyone drops everything when you walk by. I don't see it. I don't like you. And Magnus let the elastic snap, and Wes said, I don't like you either.

At the party, I got very drunk. Someone handed me a joint. I had my arms up, I was dancing. Wes was in my periphery. His hair was long to his ribs. He was in the dark suit he always wore, I loved that slender dark suit, and then he was in our murky front hallway, and then he was leaving. I wanted to say goodnight to Wes, I moved to follow him, but then Magnus was behind me with his hands bracketing my hip bones, he was speaking into my ear, his meaty breath. Magnus was saying, You're a happy person. I was saying, I'm not actually. I'm not a happy person at all, and I stepped out of his grip. And then Magnus was saying, I want to play you something. I want to play you the song I'm thinking of using for your entrance, but it's too loud in here, and he indicated the doors to our bedrooms, and I led him to mine. Magnus closed the door behind us. He looked around, he said, What a hectic bedroom, then he made a gun out of his fingers and mock blew his brains out. Then he kissed me, a brief, hard kiss, and I stepped back. Don't do that, I said, what the fuck. I heard myself swear and I snapped my elastic. Magnus asked me if I was alright, and I said, fine, wasted, fine, play the song. Magnus put his phone inside the bowl on my bedside table. First, he dumped the bowl. Coins, rings, bus pass, hair ties, condoms, aspirin, band-aids, library card. Magnus told me Francis Bacon's favourite part of the body was the mouth. Francis Bacon wanted to paint mouths the way Monet painted sunsets. Then Magnus played a song by the Magnetic Fields. We just stood there in my bedroom and listened to the song. Magnus said, You look worried, and I said, I was born worried. Magnus said, You're so interesting, Mona. There's so much pressure in my industry to be interesting. Tell me every interesting thing you know. And I said, I know this song is boring. He laughed which made his eyes tear up. I went for the doorknob, but Magnus was there first. Magnus was smiling, then he said, What are you, a hundred pounds soaking wet?, and he lifted me high in the air. Then he placed me down on the floor and pulled me into him, I could feel his muscles through his clothes, and then he held me by my jaw, and licked the right side of my face. I pulled back to see if he was joking, lost my balance, and fell onto my bed. The room spun, and I tried to get my feet on to the floor. Magnus dragged my dresser across the door frame, saying, So we don't get interrupted, and then he was on top of me, saying my name, moving his hands over my body. He was unbuttoning the front of my dress, which left me naked, and I was saying, Hold on, hold on. I could feel my hands swatting the air, but slowly like I was moving gravity, and I was saying, Hold on, but the rule, fucking don't. And Magnus was unbuckling his belt, the metal hit my thigh and then pinched it, and then he had his zipper down. I tried to cross my right leg over me, but he pressed it back and down and open, it hurt and I heard myself cry out, but he was too strong, my mouth was buried in his chest, and he was pushing himself into me.

When he was done, he said he wasn't sure I had what it took to play Medea. He wanted to be sure about me, but he just wasn't yet. There was still time for him to recast. Think of next week as your test week, Magnus said, and he dealt with his zipper and his belt. The other young women in the class would die to play that part. They had the mettle, the heart, the guts. He would have each of them memorize the role, in case. I don't know, Magnus said, I don't know. You're like Michelle Pfeiffer in *Scarface*. Are you terrible or a revelation? I don't know, he said again. Maybe I did have it in me. We'd see what I could deliver. If I did deliver, he'd be able to help me once I graduated. He couldn't talk about it yet, but major planets were on the move. Magnus picked up his phone, checked it, and put it in his pocket. Under his breath he said, You girls and your Anaïs Nin. Then with his large hand, he swept everything back into the bowl on my side table. He told me tenderly, You look like a corpse, Mona, get dressed.

From my bed, I could hear Magnus saying goodnight to the remaining guests, telling Ani to be sure to blow out the candles, and keep an eye on me, I was wasted. Enough time passed, I knew Magnus was gone. I buttoned my dress, he had ripped my dress, I skidded across one of the loose buttons, and it felt like a shard of glass slicing my foot, I heard myself wince, I grabbed a jacket to cover the rip in my dress, and I went to the all-night drugstore for the morning-after pill. On the way, I sucked the ends of my fingers, and wiped away the mascara and the salt on my face. I felt his come spill down my legs. I used my dress as a rag against the insides of my thighs. I held back my hair and vomited into the bushes. I stopped every fifty feet or so. The garbage was being collected. Overflowing cans lined the sidewalk. A couple of men walked by me and spat on the ground. One of them had a neck tattoo that read LIQUID EYES. The all-night drugstore was lit brightly like a casino. I pulled off my jacket and lay it over my head, tenting my face. I stood at the counter while the pharmacist ignored me. He came over and I asked him for the morning-after pill. He turned away without saying anything. A few minutes later, he pushed a small stapled bag at me, said the instructions were in the bag. I opened the bag and swallowed the pill. I paid. I told the pharmacist that he had a problem, and I wasn't it. I blocked my pubic bone with my palm. Everywhere, I hurt. I snapped the elastic on my wrist. I pulled my jacket down on to my shoulders. I grabbed a hand mirror and looked at myself. My eyes were wet and black, my pupils were giant black discs, and my lipstick was smeared in such an ugly way, I looked mouthless. I snapped the elastic again. I told the pharmacist that I hadn't washed my hair or masturbated in three weeks. I walked into a nearby aisle and looked for something disgusting. I opened a bag of Doritos, they were like glass in my throat, I couldn't stomach them. Then I said every foul word I could think of until a security guard was standing in front of me. He hooked his arms beneath mine and deposited me in front of the drugstore. Ani was there on the sidewalk, she had been looking for me.

When we ran out of hot water, Ani boiled more and filled the bathtub. She wanted me to go to the hospital. She wanted me to go to the police. She wanted me to go to the director of the school. I will, I said. Promise me, she said. No, I said. I can't.

Paul happened to be in the city for a screening of *Daughter* the night *Medea* was closing. He missed the show because the events conflicted, but we met afterward for a late dinner. Paul was already sitting in the restaurant when I arrived, his back to the door. He wore a dark-blue sweater, his white hair neatly combed. I had not seen him in six months, not since I had come home for Natasha and Judd's wedding. Before approaching the table, I watched Paul for a minute. I liked seeing him alone with himself. He was a serious person, concentrated. I felt that with me, the weather system would change, my presence would agitate him. Paul was studying the wine list. I kissed his cheek and sat down across from him. You smell like shampoo, Paul said. My hair was still dripping from the shower. I apologized for being late. I asked Paul how the event had gone, and he said, Good, fine, good, it's a good fucking movie. It is, I agreed. Paul seemed happy, and I told him so. I am happy, he said, it's been a long time. Paul asked if I wanted a glass of sparkling wine. No, thank you. The waitress came and Paul made a comment to her about her beauty, the women in this city were the most beautiful women in the world, Paul said. Paul told the waitress that she was too beautiful to be working in a restaurant. Surely, she was an actress. The waitress was an actress. They laughed at that, and Paul said, I knew it. Good for you. Paul ordered a bottle of red wine, and then he returned his attentions to me. He looked at me with love, but I knew that Paul loved whoever happened to be across from him. He asked whether I was sure I could miss the closing night party. Yes, I'm sure, it's just a party. He'd heard from Cherry that the director was a big deal, she'd done some reading up on him, it looked like he was about to do a major movie. Paul asked if I shouldn't be networking, making an impression. No, I said, the director already knows what I can do. And besides, I didn't bother explaining to Paul, Magnus flew out immediately after closing, the red-eye to London. He'd left his business card in my dressing room and written his cell number across the back and below it, the word *REVELATION*. Paul and I drank our wine. I ordered French fries and mayonnaise, and Paul asked if I didn't want anything else. I knew Magnus had not given me an infection or a disease. I told Ani the battery of tests was all I could do for now. I told Ani, I'll be fine. I still had a bruise on my left thigh. It was grey now, nearly gone, it looked like a nuclear cloud. Paul told me he was finally working on something decent. I said, That's good. He had finished two other novels, but Cherry had called them small fish, maudlin, pornography. He'd locked them in a storage unit, nearly shot them to pieces. Judd said Cherry was too possessive, she wasn't even in publishing for God's sake and she was steering him toward obscurity. Paul and Judd had argued. Paul told Judd it was with Cherry he had published *Daughter*. Judd told Paul it was with *Natasha* that he'd *written* it. Anyway, I wasn't invited to the wedding, Paul said, I hadn't expected to be. I'm happy for Judd. Natasha is brilliant, Judd will never be bored. After a moment, Paul said, you look tired, Mona, thin. He asked if I was still working at the go-kart track, and I said yes, then I travelled in my mind to the evening bus and then to the coat check with my stuffed bra and tight jeans, sitting with a carpet over my knees because it was so cold in that room. Paul said I was like a sleepwalker, what is it. Sorry. Paul asked if it was too much to be working on top of going to school, the program was so demanding, and I said, no, it was fine, manageable. He said, You don't seem like yourself, Mona, you seem flat, what is it. And I almost told Paul because I could, because he was like me, he wouldn't do anything about it. Then Paul glanced under the table at my boots and my purse, he asked if I needed money, and I said no. Then Paul said, Jesus, Mona. He was looking at my left wrist, where I had worn the elastic for the last six weeks, it was red and raw and swollen. What happened, he said, that looks so sore. I lied to Paul and said it was stage makeup, I had forgotten to wash it off. Jesus, he said again, and sat back, I can see why they call it the best school in the country. Then he asked about the play, and I said, *Medea*, well, as you know, it's about a woman who murders her kids to spite her husband who, and before I could finish, a woman in a jean jacket appeared at our table. She was not much older than me. Paul got to his feet, I could see his chest flare, and he and the woman grinned at each other. Then Paul said, Mona, I want you to meet Lee.

.   .   .

That was the night Ani and Wes got together, at the closing party for *Medea*.

. . .

I lied to you, Ani was saying. We were standing together in front of the theatre. It was our graduation night. The air was hot. People were out. The moon was a smudge, it looked coated in Vaseline. Cars passed us and honked. Ani and I spun for the passing cars. Ani dipped me, I closed my eyes, let my arms go lifeless, felt the top of my head drag along the pavement. Ani was wearing a low-cut ballgown she had pulled from the costume room, the sweep of her dark hair cut bluntly just below her ears. She pulled two cigarettes from between her breasts, put them in her mouth, lit them and passed one to me. She held my shoulders and then turned me to face the glass. The party inside shook the glass. The lights strobed. I could see Wes in jagged flashes of white light, he was dancing, he had shaved his head and bleached his scalp, he looked like a dandelion going to seed, he was off to one side of the large room and he was dancing as if he was losing his mind. The song was "Tainted Love." Think about it, Ani was saying. He didn't stay over once. We had a relationship because he was too polite not to. I was wearing Ani's Frankie Goes to Hollywood T-shirt, black tights and black pumps. My eyes were lined with black liquid liner. I looked up at Ani, but she zeroed in on the room, on Wes appearing and disappearing with the pulsing light, so I did too. Eventually, she said, I don't lie.

I know that, I said.

You don't lie.

I don't.

I was in pain. Ani exhaled and smoke drifted over our faces. I'm not in pain anymore.

Then she said, The night Wes broke up with me, I told you he'd withheld the name of the other woman, he'd said it was pointless to tell me, he could never be with her anyway. I lied to you, Mona. Wes told me it was you, he was in love with you. And then Ani said, Please forgive me. Please forgive me, Mona. Wes thought you'd had an affair with Magnus. And I never corrected him.

.   .   .

Natasha was lying next to me in my bed and she was talking to me. You know everybody gives grief this bad name, Natasha was saying to me. I had my eyes open, my back to her. Wes was in the kitchen, he was cooking. Everything he did, he did noisily. He had left the crib at his studio. He made a box and now the baby's ashes were in the box, I had put the box on my side of the closet. Grief is the worst thing, Natasha was saying to me, but it is not only that. My mother was wearing her fur coat. Her perfume filled the room, she smelled like the airport. It's freezing in here, she'd said when she first came in, it's a meat locker, and Wes explained that the heat had been out for a day, but it was fixed now and it should feel warm again soon enough. Sorry about that, Tash, Wes said to my mother, and they held each other for a long time in our kitchen, and I heard Wes make a gulping sound. I looked up at our ceiling. I could see my breath. Wes had painted the ceiling when we first moved in, but it was soft and green again. The water stain was spreading slowly from the corner of the ceiling.

My mother touched my back gently. I was separate from my mother, I was separate from Wes. My mother's platinum-blond hair was done, her makeup. She would leave the tan powder from her foundation on Wes's pillow. She was saying, Grief can be generative as well, Mona. A lot can come of grief. I had pill bottles beside my bed, half-empty cups of tea. My milk had come in and it was very painful. I had to put compresses on my breasts to discourage the milk, I had to take pills to tell my body it had no one to feed. I was separate from my body, I hated my body, I wanted my body to die. I went to the bathroom, I cried, I looked out the window, I cried. You could see the lake from our apartment, a skim of ice had formed over the water. The sky was overcast, a dirty grey, the trees were skeletal. At night, I took the last of the morphine from the hospital, I drank it down with Scotch. It wasn't even darkness I entered. It was a nothing state. Wes said, Be careful, Mona. Natasha had brought a soup. She said it was mostly okra. She said it wouldn't taste good, but it would help me get my strength back. She said I had to try to eat. Come now, Mona, she said, and she touched my back again. She fell silent. Her breath was thick and I thought she might have fallen asleep. Then she said, It wasn't your fault. You didn't do anything wrong, Mona. The baby was sick, there was nothing you could have done for him. And now Wes was in the bedroom and he was kneeling beside me with a panicked look. Natasha was sitting upright, she was apologizing to Wes. I could hear myself like an animal trapped in the room. Then I was saying, It's okay, it's okay. Eventually Wes backed out of the bedroom and I could hear him again in the kitchen, moving things around. Then Natasha told me, Judd sends his love. That's nice, I said. I didn't want to see Judd. I didn't even want to see Natasha. I hardly wanted to see Wes. Natasha stormed the place, Wes would say to me once she was gone. She was so worried about you.

Paul wrote. Mona, no doubt you have to deal with the present, but you have to do so in the context of your total life which includes so many good things. This is a test of your and Wes's strength. Fortunately, you two have resources. Good days follow bad. I know this to be true.

Some nights, I would call Paul from our bed. I would pull the heavy covers over my head and I'd listen to Paul describe what he saw in his immediate view and what he had done that day and what he planned to do the day following, and it was like listening to a list, the list of what the living did.

I would tell Paul things I could not tell Wes because I was already such a burden to Wes, I was already so disfigured and ugly with need. You should leave me, I would beg Wes. I told Paul that grief was immovable and it had no dimension, it was just there, and it lived in my throat and in my chest and in my organs. I would talk in an almost-whisper to Paul. I told Paul that I didn't know if I wanted the grief to go away because it was *of* the baby, it was my only form of closeness to him. And then I would peel back the covers to try to get my breath, and I would look around our bedroom, and think, Paul has never been to our apartment, does he even know where I live.

Juliet flew in. It was a sixteen-hour flight. She sat cross-legged on the floor of our bedroom and unzipped her suitcase, everything in it was rolled. She gave me Japanese candy and Wes comic books. Wes leaned against the bedroom wall with his arms loose and free. Wes thanked Juliet for coming all this way. He hugged Juliet and left the bedroom. Juliet told me she had heard that jet lag is your soul trying to catch up to your body. Juliet told me the day I lost my baby, she had a miscarriage. The same day, well not the same day because of the time zones, but the same day. Today for you is tomorrow for me, Juliet said. Your loss occurred on a Friday night and mine on a Saturday afternoon, but they occurred at the same time in our bodies. Then Juliet had Wes set up the TV at the foot of our bed. Wes wound and unwound cables, and when Juliet asked if he wanted to watch the movie too, he said, Ah, no, thank you, I've already seen *Ghost*, he joked with Juliet, and without kissing me, Wes looked in my general direction, he held up his hands as if to say *sorry* or *what*, but I did not have it in me to decipher Wes, and Wes went into the living room. He slept on the couch. There was a single blanket on the couch, a glass of water on the floor. I would pass by Wes's area when I went to the bathroom. I did not know which one of us was the intruder. Every day, I asked Juliet to show me photos of her son. Every day, she lied and said she didn't have any. I tugged on the ends of Juliet's clothes. It will happen for you, Juliet was saying. But I had no mind for the future. I wanted only what I had. I explained the feeling to Juliet. I could not get my breath. I showed Juliet. I sat up in bed. I made my hand flat like a seal to indicate where my lungs stopped filling. My chest was tight. I had to sigh constantly to release the pressure in my chest. Juliet said, you have to cry. I've already cried, I told Juliet, I cried when Natasha came. Then Juliet sat behind me. She put her arms around me but they were the arms of a new mother holding her son. I repositioned myself in the bed. Juliet put pillows behind us. There, she said. She described the wall as frigid. She described the apartment as Muscovite. She'd forgotten how cold it got here. You're living in a Russian novel. Is there no comfort? There, Juliet said again and she leaned against the pillow, motioned I do the same, and Juliet handed me her phone. I swiped at her son. I swiped at his perfect, open face and his small, powerful body. I sighed. I closed my eyes. My mind was alert. My mind was nocturnal. I went over the days leading up to the stillbirth. If I hadn't had dinner with Paul. If I hadn't walked home with Wes. If I hadn't flown. Small details came back to me. The nurse must have returned her pen to her pocket without clicking it closed as there were blue pen marks all around the pocket of her white lab coat. If the nurse had clicked her pen closed. I needed to sequence the events that led to the stillbirth. When Juliet asked me a question or Wes entered the room, I was set back and forced to start the sequence anew. Juliet cleaned the windows with vinegar. She held up takeout menus. I watched Juliet go over the floor with a broom. She swept in sections. Juliet straightened the room, she tucked in my bedcovers. When I rested, I could hear Juliet leave the bedroom and delicately close the bedroom and bathroom doors behind her. She called home. Her husband would answer then turn the phone on their son, and I could hear the surrender in Juliet's voice. She did not belong to herself. She belonged to him. It's okay, I would say to Juliet when she crept back into the room. I told her I was sorry about her miscarriage. She said, It's nothing like what you had to go through, God. And then Juliet said she was sorry, she shouldn't be the one crying, I should be the one crying, but I was not crying and this was disturbing her, the way I was behaving. You have to get less sad, Mona, Juliet said. Juliet who was of the earth but also of the gods. Juliet never adjusted to our time zone. She was with me for four, maybe five nights. We talked through the night the way we did in Spain. When daylight invaded the room, Juliet pulled the curtains closed. Then she hung a blanket from the curtain rod. She blackened the room so we were just voices. Cherry's name came up and Juliet said, She can fuck off and die. Then Paul's name came up and I felt Juliet's body relax beside mine. Then Natasha's name came up, and Juliet said, She's such an enigma.

No, I said to Juliet. She's the most deliberate person in our life. Look at how close we got to being motherless.

Juliet left. She called from the airport. *Hey*. Juliet told me she was eating a sandwich with her gloves on. She told me she was famished. We ate nothing, Juliet said. What the fuck. She told me there was some guy who kept looking over at her and if he approached her table, she was going to flip it. She said the table was not bolted down. You would think a table in the airport would be bolted down. Juliet said she was looking through the glass at the airplanes taxiing and she felt this combination of words misrepresented both airplanes and taxis. It was like combining animals. Juliet told me we knew too little about our mother and too much about our father. She did not know where this left us. Guessing, I answered. Juliet said there was something so beautiful about the airport. She could miss her flight for the beauty. She said it took all her willpower not to launch her table through the glass. She wanted to hear the shattering sound. She wanted to feel the air rush in. Why is everything so separate? Juliet asked. Listen to me, Juliet said. You fuck me up. Then I overheard Juliet order a whiskey, neat. She had a Xanax for the flight.

Wes said, you have to talk to me.

There is nothing to say.

I don't know how to help you.

I don't want your help.

Wes was parking in the underground lot. We were downtown again. He wound the car down and down and down the ramp until he found a spot on the lowest level. He backed up the car into a space and turned off the engine. He put his hand over mine and said, If doom were a place. And then Wes said, Let's go. Wes would wait for me while I saw the grief counsellor at the hospital. Our midwife had set up the appointment, Wes had called our midwife. He thought I was asleep. I could hear Wes on the phone in the living room. She's not improving, Wes was saying, she's already a person who gets depressed. She's a depressive person. She said I should leave her, she said I should leave her because she has already left herself. She said there's no point in me sticking around. Then I could tell Wes was listening closely and arrangements were being made, he was writing things down, there was a world on the other side of the door. It was my turn to talk to the midwife. It is a free service, our midwife was explaining in her measured voice, it is only a half hour, and then she softened, it is at a different hospital from where you had the baby. Our midwife had missed my stillbirth because she'd had to leave a few hours into my labour, she kept checking her pager, and though she did not say it, I knew she'd had to leave to attend to a live birth. Even though it was lightless in the parking lot, I wore the sunglasses from Natasha's cataract surgery, they were wide black glasses that were meant to fit over other glasses. Wes and I were below ground. He held my hand and we entered the elevator. He pressed the correct buttons, we rode upward and when the doors opened, he led me down hallways, making lefts then rights like some kind of joke. How could anyone get well in a hospital, it was frantic like the stock exchange. The grief counsellor sat in her packed, dim office. I took the only other chair, the chair opposite hers, but it was too close. When I broke down and could not stop, she told me to place my feet firmly on the floor. My feet were already firmly on the floor. Can no one do anything for me, can no one say anything to change my mind. *Change my mind.* Then she would say, Let go and let God, and I would say, Okay, okay. Afterward Wes and I would have to make the long way back to our car. I felt what it was to carry oneself, and that Wes and I were just carrying ourselves, nothing more.

.　.　.

I looked down at my empty, distended stomach, and I told Ani I was sorry, I couldn't see her yet.

Remember, Ani said over the phone, when we were Harold and Maude for Halloween? I remember, Harold, I said. When I couldn't reach Ani, my call went to her voice mail. She had made it that Lionel Richie song.

Hello, is it me you're looking for?

I started to call Ani just to listen to that song.

THREE

It was March when I finally stopped bleeding. I had hemorrhaged two weeks after the stillbirth and lost a third of my blood volume. Wes and I were in Chinatown when it happened. Juliet had just flown home, I had just seen the grief counsellor, and Wes said, Let's go do a normal thing, so we'd driven into Chinatown for noodles. It was night and Chinatown was brightly lit and crowded with people, it had a carnival atmosphere. I was stepping over a snowbank to get back into the car when it started. We were in Emergency for hours before a bed became free. Over and over, Wes and I had to tell the story of the stillbirth. In the hospital room, Wes slept upright in a chair beside me. The nurses said they gave us a private room because we had been through so much already. Wes had a flip phone and he would talk to Natasha most days. She would update Juliet and Ani. Paul called. Wes told Paul that the IV bothered me more than anything else. It was in the vein next to my wrist bone. In Emergency, the nurse had said, your veins are tricky. She'd said make a fist and she tapped my forearm looking for a vein, the vein in my wrist was the only one she could find. I'm sorry, the nurse said, I know it's in a bad spot, and then she directed the needle into my vein and taped it into place. Wes and I spent entire days and nights together in that large empty room, not knowing how long we would be kept there. I wheeled my IV from the bed to the bathroom to deal with my blood. I relayed the amounts of blood to the nurses, and they noted it, that was what I was supposed to do, bleed and then report it. In the bathroom, I avoided the sight of myself. One evening, the doctor came in to restate the treatment plan to me and to Wes. We are keeping a close eye on things, the doctor said, we are trying to let her body take care of it. Then she paused, and I thought she might tell us more about my condition, and instead the doctor asked me if I wasn't Paul Dean's daughter. Yes, I am. Your face was on the side of that building a couple of years ago, the doctor said, a theatre, I think. Anyway, some of us were wondering if you weren't Paul Dean's daughter. Well, I am. The doctor smiled. Then she asked me if the book, *Daughter*, was based on me, and I said, No, no, it's not, it's fiction, he made her up. But the daughter, the doctor continued as if we were talking at a party, anyway the daughter he describes in the book, she's a dead ringer for you. And Wes was on his feet asking the doctor if he could please speak with her in the corridor. I could hear Wes in the corridor. His voice was raised and it was reverberating. We have been here for a week and is the plan to watch my wife bleed to death while you ask her personal questions, Wes was saying this to the doctor, because if that is the plan you should let me know so I can take her to a different hospital with a better plan. When Wes came back into the hospital room, he found me unconscious. I could hear the voices before I could open my eyes, and then there were a few doctors leaning over my bed, saying Mona, Mona, one was shining a narrow light into my pupils, giving me instructions, look this way and that way, Mona, and then they were lowering my gown, they were listening to my heart. I was rushed into surgery which was being rushed into nowhere.

When we got home, we had bouquets of flowers rotting through the apartment. There was an underwater smell, the smell of a swamp. I had to move very slowly while my blood did the work of regenerating itself. No sudden movements, Wes said, and he always had a hand on me. I had to keep my head low and angled forward, I got dizzy very easily and was embarrassed by my frailty. When I showered, Wes was on the other side of the curtain, leaning against the edge of the sink, his ankles crossed, asking every few minutes how I was doing in there. The moment I turned off the water, Wes was there to pull the curtain open, to help me step my vile body over the lip of the tub and into a towel. We'd stand together cowering in the fog. I still avoided the sight of my face. There was relief at being returned to our privacy. Every night in the hospital, the lights would flick on, a tray would be wheeled in, and a nurse would say my name, then shake me awake to check my vitals. Blood pressure, temperature, pulse. One night when the nurse had left the large room to continue her rounds, but Wes and I were still stunned awake, Wes told me he was sorry to raise anything right now, but he needed to talk. He was worried about money. He had his parka draped over him, his legs jutting out from the chair he'd spent over a week sitting in. Wes straightened, rubbed his hands over his thighs, he dropped his head. The gallery had been a mistake, he hated to admit it, he hadn't thought it through in a realistic way, he'd been in a fantasy state when he'd conceived of the gallery, the gallery coincided with our engagement, our marriage, with a time when all Wes could see was possibility. He had no idea life could feel so future-less. Sorry, Wes said, but you know what I mean, I don't have to explain that feeling to you. He went on. He couldn't sup-port us with his art, the return was just too meagre. He knew his art wasn't for everyone. Water, Wes said to himself, only water is for everyone. Anyway, he knew his installation art was not. I listened to Wes. He spoke methodically, fasten-ing one thought to the next. Wes sorted out his chaos in the private corners of himself, and then came back to me once he'd reached some new insight, some resolve, but only then. I'd seen his apartment when we were at theatre school, it was after graduation, stopping to make out on our way to his apartment, my legs hooking around his waist, his body pressing us into some chain-link fence, it was in an industrial area, no other students lived in that area, I was shocked when I first saw where Wes lived. I called his place the bunker. The bunker was where Wes sorted through himself. Far underground, deep inside concrete, behind a metal door. Until then, Wes was out of reach. In that large hospital room, I had to smother the urge to console Wes, to interrupt him and assure him that I could support us, he didn't need to worry, he could continue with his art practice at the very least. But I knew any assurances from me would come through as false, we would waste time on them, on my empty words, on my pathetic habit of trying to make things better. I was bleeding in the artificial darkness of a downtown hospital room, I couldn't see that far ahead, I couldn't promise a thing, I had no idea who I would be when we left this room. I've made a decision, Mona, Wes said then. I'm going back into acting. I was a fucking hothead when I quit. I didn't recognize what good fortune I had. I wasn't practical. Then Wes let out a small laugh, And I don't want to be an exterminator. I don't want to spend my life killing things.

I told Wes I was sorry I had withdrawn from him after the stillbirth. I could hardly understand what was happening inside my mind or my body, both seemed to be working against me. I told Wes about the sequencing. The concentration it required was excruciating and I still hadn't gotten to the end. I lied to Wes and told him I would stop. And Wes said, I don't think I can sit here any longer. He got to his feet, swivelled his torso. Maybe I hadn't spoken my thoughts aloud. Wes climbed into the hospital bed and tried to extend his body beside mine. My IV was in my right arm so there was no risk of disturbing it, ripping the needle from my vein, but I kept my body very still and made my breath shallow, just enough. Wes faced me and immediately I felt him lulled into sleep. The grey wall, a semigloss. A locker for our things. What things? Factual voices over the intercom announcing levels of emergency. This went on through the night. Sometime later, Wes stirred. The sun was coming up. The light against the window was cold and blue. Wes climbed carefully out of the hospital bed, checked for his wallet and asked me if I wanted anything. I shook my head no. Wes left the room. A siren wailed. My IV was a tendril depositing a solution into my body. It looked like a line in when it was a line out. In slow, persistent drips, my IV was withdrawing my body. The nurse would switch out the plastic bags and less of my body would remain and I would thank the nurse. Outside, a truck engine rumbled to life. Wes's footfall was so familiar to me. I could see him through walls. Wes felt that by answering the question of his future, he had answered that question for me. He meant to comfort me, but I was alone with my questions, and I wanted to be. I could not stand another set of probing eyes. Wes came back into the room eating a Twinkie from the vending machine, carrying a Styrofoam cup of Red Rose tea. I smiled at him. He stood by the window and looked out. He could have been anyone.

Once we were home, Natasha visited nearly every afternoon. Wes had a key made for her so she could just let herself into the apartment. She was always done up when she came over to see me. She was Marilyn Monroe had Marilyn Monroe driven a sedan and worked at a radio station. She had taken a leave from work. I would hear Natasha in the hallway greeting our neighbours, and I would hide behind our door.

I was terrified of seeing anyone, of encountering anyone I knew, because I would have to explain what had happened to my body and my face. Natasha would tell me, after I had recovered, that during those two months, I was a pale-green colour, it was an unnatural colour, it was the colour of sickness, she had never seen that colour before on a living face. You looked like you'd been poisoned, Natasha would say. She would sit across from me at the small table by our front window and watch me spoon soup into my mouth until my stomach clamped shut. She would tell me our building should be condemned, we should complain to the city, the foyer alone was a death trap.

Wes returned to the world, to the world of people and cars and jobs and weather and time. He was on the phone in the living room setting up meetings with agencies and then he was signed to an agent, a big one, and soon, he was auditioning, he was running lines in our living room, he was a haunted detective, he was a hit man, he was a dying husband, a drug addict. Wes was a man playing other men. It was a crisis that had led Wes to quit acting. After playing Hamlet, Wes told me that he had spooked himself. It was a problem of re-entry, Wes said, he couldn't re-enter the atmosphere. He had decided he needed to do something that lay outside of his physical body, something with scale, something tangible, and so he turned his full attention to installation art. But now, Wes had reversed the crisis that acting had caused within him. He had come up with a way to be. He had exited our grief. I admired Wes and I resented him. I resented his health. I would watch Wes in his dark clothes leave the apartment in the morning and then come back from set hours later, drop his keys on the couch, his supple mouth around the news, whatever the news, and then his long, purposeful body striding into our galley kitchen, opening the fridge, rummaging through it, the projection of light on his face, I found him beautiful, I wanted to know him but I couldn't, I was still at the other end of a tunnel.

One afternoon, Natasha brought Judd's dog with her. I could hear his claws scrape against the cracked marble stairwell on their way up to the apartment, his heavy breathing as he strained against the leash. Hunk was a Rottweiler with a handsome, boulder-sized head. I can't very well leave him in the car, Natasha said, gripping his leather collar, he'll destroy it. I ran my hands through his short oily coat. He hustled his massive, shining body between our rooms, salivating and knocking things to the ground. Hunk, my mother said, get a hold of yourself. Hunk climbed up onto my bed, circled once, then let his legs go weak as if he'd been shot. He lay beside me and panted there. Natasha was in the bedroom too, she was going through my drawers. She was holding up my clothing, piece by piece, asking what she could give away. That, that, that, I would say to my mother, and Natasha would drop my clothes into an open garbage bag.

Beside me, Hunk sounded as if he was inflating something. I watched his ribs rise and fall. I felt the heat of him, his bulk, dense as cement. Outside, Judd waited in the car. Whenever Natasha went anywhere, Judd drove her and parked close by and he sat in the driver's seat and he read. Judd waited for my mother, my mother could take as long as she needed, Judd would be there when she exited our building, Judd would feel Natasha's approach, look up and see her, he would lean over and open the passenger side door for her and she would fold her body in beside his. Natasha was lying about Hunk destroying the car. Judd was in the car. Natasha knew that only an animal draws us out when we are hurting. Natasha was cunning. I got my secrecy from Natasha. I got everything but my face from Natasha. In my bedroom, I watched my mother closely, my newly married mother dressed for the occasion of visiting her sick daughter. She was radiant, she was helping me, it was so simple, these afternoon hours together. I wanted to ask my mother why she told me about trying to kill herself when I was twelve. For years, I lived in fear that it could happen again, that at any moment, my mother could break apart and take her own life. I lived inside my mother's uneven view of the world, the volatility of her heart, and it made me nervous and watchful. Everything I did, I did to please her, to undo her pain. I shadowed her. I hated to be away from my mother, I constantly pictured finding her dead. I thought back to Cherry on the island making rain with her hands, laughing at what a dour child I was, *Tragedia*, the nickname she and Paul had given to me. Juliet and I were asleep downstairs when my mother swallowed the pills in her bathroom. She then went out to the car. The car was in the garage. She was going to run the car. Instead, Natasha drove herself to Emergency. She nearly got there, but lost consciousness on the way, and veered into a guardrail. Now, my mother was knotting the black garbage bag filled with my things, she was telling me I should rest. I felt I knew what it was to find yourself living in a flat world, and having nothing left to summon, searching for the will to go on and not finding it, even in the face of your daughter. I forgave my mother for what she did, and for planting the idea of suicide in my mind.

Later that afternoon, after I'd slept, I found Natasha on the couch in the living room, marking up a manuscript. I asked her what it was and she said, Oh nothing, and she slipped the manuscript back into its envelope. Then she said, your father asked Judd and me to read his latest. She saw the surprise on my face and said, I know. Then she said, I don't know why that man hasn't published in twenty years. Must be one of the conditions of his captivity.

Natasha spoke this last bit to herself but also to Paul. She had never fully abandoned the habit of speaking to Paul. When they were married, Natasha and Paul spoke continuously. Their marriage was one long conversation. Natasha felt independent in the marriage. She felt that around her burned a circle and Paul was perpetually seeking admission. He wanted to step over her high flames. Paul would come to Natasha for her opinion on a line, should he word it this way or that way, her take on a character, whether he was on to something. Paul wanted to be soothed, but Natasha was more a surgeon than a nurse. She was candid, busy, a mother. She wanted some free time to smoke and look at the clouds. She wanted to walk at night, be alone with her thoughts. She had no time for idle emotion. There was just too much to do. Tersely, Natasha told Paul to hand over his pages. At first, he hovered, but when Paul saw the edits Natasha was making to *Daughter*, he guarded the door instead. The children were afraid Natasha had fallen ill. They saw her infrequently and when they did the eyes that looked at them were not their mother's eyes. Natasha slept in her chair. She slept in her dress. Behind the closed door, Natasha could see and hear the novel. She just needed time to get it down. Paul left trays of food at the door. Natasha ignored the food. She was in communion with her mind. Natasha told Paul she was working with the speed of an animal being chased by a larger animal and the larger animal was time. Keep the children away from me, Natasha told Paul. I am, he said. I don't know how long I can stand being apart from them, she told Paul. Natasha believed in Paul's gift, but fatally, Paul did not. He was an insecure man. As a result, his sentences were insecure. Natasha secured Paul's sentences. Paul pursued the guns, the fights, the infidelities to make a legend of himself. His experience of catastrophe was limited to the performance of catastrophe. The fights were rigged. The target an outline. The infidelities empty. None of it was ever truly felt. Men did not know how to enter strangeness the way women did. Natasha could feel how much Paul needed her, he needed the very centre of her. Her marrow, her sex, her soul. Whatever you wanted to call it, Paul tried to fuck himself into it, then talk himself into it, he was still pursuing Natasha's centre.

I went into the kitchen. I did not know what to do in the kitchen. Hunk was pushing his muzzle into my hip, he was whining and barking. I must have started to cry. It was that I hated to wake up, I hated to be awake. Then Natasha was there, she was telling Hunk to stop being melodramatic, and then she was speaking to me. You know, Natasha was saying, they say that grief is love with nowhere to go. I think that's true at first, but then, Natasha was saying, I think that undersells love. Love finds its rightful place.

.   .   .

Ani was on the phone. I was reading again. I had my back against the bedroom wall, a pillow propped behind me. On this day, it was raining, Ani was saying, I love this Biblical weather, it was raining so hard that our walls were wet, I

could hear the rain outside surging into the storm gutters,
I had to speak loudly to Ani, I had to speak over the rain. I
was telling Ani that Virginia Woolf wrote in her diary that
behind her characters lay beautiful caves, and that the caves
held her characters' humanity and their humour, and that
one day the caves would connect. *One day the caves would
connect*—I quoted Virginia Woolf to Ani. The tragic thing,
I said to Ani, the tragic thing is that she believed this for
her characters, but she couldn't believe this for herself. She
couldn't extend this faith in things to herself. Writing could
sustain her for only so long before the world rushed in. Writing could fix her life until it couldn't. Then I told Ani that
what happened to me sounded more like a gothic poem than
like my life, that after my baby's stillbirth my body would fill
itself with new blood. Then I told Ani, *Ophelia* autocorrects to
hemophilia. Ophelia. Hemophilia. Blood just giving of itself,
refusing to clot. Hard to ignore. Ophelia and Virginia Woolf
both ended their lives in water. Hard to ignore. Guess how
many times Ophelia is spoken about after her funeral scene?
And at that, Ani blew a hot zero into the receiver, and then
she said, You sound strong, my girl, you sound strong for
the first time in four months.

One day the caves would connect.

.   .   .

A month later, Paul sent an email to me and Juliet. It was his seventieth birthday, and he wrote to tell us that he and Cherry were up on the island even though it was still cold, it was early in the season, the ice floes were gone, but just. Paul thanked me for my note. I'd wished Paul a happy birthday. I'd quoted Rachel Cusk quoting D. H. Lawrence: *I don't feel I am getting older, I feel I am getting closer*. Picking up on this word *closer*, Paul wrote that he had never felt closer to us, and he thanked me and Juliet for our friendship. We knew him, Paul wrote, in ways no one else did, and for that he was grateful. It made life far less lonely. Paul ended his email by saying that it had been one hell of a boat trip out to the island. Here I am, Paul wrote, having lived to tell the tale. Beneath Paul's note was a photo of Paul, that furtive look in his eyes, he was smiling in his sheepish way, he'd had a piece of his rib in his jaw ever since his jaw had been smashed in a fight so his jaw was a bit off, he was wearing a blue wool hat that I recognized from my childhood, and a quilted flannel jacket, his skin was ruddy from the cold, clean air, his skin was pockmarked by the acne of his youth, the acne that had sent him into the boxing ring, the acne that had sent him into his bedroom, behind a locked door, to read, and then to write. Paul talked about writing as being in conversation with God, when it was working, Paul said, he was in conversation with God, when it was working, it was rapture. I noticed the stoop in Paul's shoulders, it was more pronounced than I remembered, and his frame, his broad-boned, heavyweight frame looked slighter somehow. Behind Paul lay miles of ocean. To the right of Paul was a bonfire. I could see he was at the northwestern end of the island, where the rock was at its most flat and navigable, where the sun had mostly set, where the deer had washed up the season before, where the helipad would go. Sparks flew from the bonfire and were lengthened by the slow exposure of the photo. I studied the photo. I nearly missed her, but there was a distant figure in the top right-hand corner of the photo, a tall figure who, at first, I thought must be Cherry, but then who could have taken the photo of Paul? The figure's hair was scraped back, her eyes were cast forward, it was Eva.

I wrote to Paul. Undoubtedly, he had a lot to celebrate. I thanked him for the photo. It was good to see him at long last. I hoped he was enjoying his special night with Eva and Cherry, that he felt loved by them and celebrated. I was sure, I wrote with my hands trembling, that they had feted him in high style. And then I wrote to Paul that Eva did not contact me when I lost my pregnancy. Eva did not contact me when I hemorrhaged, and nearly died. Who ignores an event like that in her sister's life? You claim that Eva is fragile, I wrote to Paul. You make this claim not to protect Eva, but to protect yourself, to protect yourself from having to confront Eva. You are intimidated by Eva, I wrote to Paul. You are intimidated by Cherry. And I pay the price for your cowardice. I went on, I laid into Paul. I told Paul that

I thought he might have given Eva some direction, it is not every day that your sister might die. I didn't expect that of Cherry, Cherry wouldn't mind if I died, she'd made her stance clear throughout my life, but I did expect that of Paul. And yet, I wrote to Paul, I could hear his excuses, I could hear his excuses because I had heard them before. Eva was her own person, she was an adult. He had no influence over her actions. He carried no sway. Then I told Paul that looking back at my apologies to Eva, my bowing down to Eva, begging Eva to come back to the relationship, made me physically sick. I couldn't even recognize myself in those emails, I was so totally in Paul's service. You would think I was the cheat, I wrote to Paul. At least I deceived no one but myself. Then I concluded my note. Alongside all the touching things that were being said that night on the island in Paul's honour, the teasing and the revelry, I hoped Paul felt some discomfort. The discomfort is your shame, I wrote to Paul. And then, again, I wished him a happy birthday.

.   .   .

Her name was Sigrid. I should have known when I walked into my living room that spring afternoon and found Natasha upright on our couch in her trench coat, she always kept her coat on in our apartment, finding Natasha immersed in Paul's manuscript, I should have known that Paul was switching his allegiances again. As he was with me, Paul was only in meaningful contact with Natasha when he was betraying his life with Cherry. He had a way of focusing his attention on one side or the other, and his focus was perfect as an algorithm. Now, seven months after his birthday, seven months after I'd sent the angry email, Paul's focus was off Cherry, Cherry's sons, and Eva, and it was back on me, Juliet and Natasha. There would be another woman involved, I knew this, and it would only be a matter of time before Paul entangled me. I wondered if the other woman was Lee. It was possible; he had loved Lee. I'd been witness to that love. I was at the bottom of my life, that was the feeling I had. It had been just over a year since the stillbirth, and I was trying to rouse myself, but I was barely back in the world. I had lists, lists beside my laptop, lists of things that I needed to do, emails I needed to write, offers I needed to respond to, and I would look at the lists and they would fracture and splinter and I couldn't begin to know what to do first, where to start, how to live. I hid this from Wes. Wes had his speed bike on his shoulder. Wes was taking the stairs two at a time. Wes was showing me something on the internet, he was learning a difficult text, he was trimming his hair over the garbage can, he was meeting Jason for a beer, he was frustrated, he was free, he was getting into a sleek black car, he was going to set. Next to Wes, I felt aimless. Wes and I used to joke about one of our classmates. We used to joke that she was a dead weight. I said about our classmate, She's like a sweater in the ocean, and Wes had laughed hard at that.

Now, I was the sweater in the ocean. My blood had done the work of regenerating itself. The problem was no longer my body and this made my inertia so much harder to explain. I didn't want Wes to lose his patience with me, I couldn't even think about what that might mean for me and my future. When Paul texted me, I was staring at my phone immobilized. I can't even remember what I was trying to do. It was Ani. Ani had given me the number for a psychiatrist she had heard was very good. I was going to call the psychiatrist, but I couldn't. I couldn't stand to explain myself again, to tell the story of what had happened, why I was so changed. I was staring at my phone, lost inside the loop of myself, when Paul texted to ask if we could meet, he needed my help, it was urgent.

I had left my bicycle chained to a post that previous winter and it had rusted through so I walked to meet Paul. It was winter, I was late. I hadn't left myself enough time to get through the thick, new snow. I was breathless when I arrived at Paul's favourite restaurant. A server I recognized from before took my heavy coat, it took too long to get the coat off my body, and I felt the server's eyes on me with something like sympathy. I straightened whatever it was that I was a wearing, a shirt of Wes's, pants of Wes's, what I always wore when I left the apartment. The shirt and the pants were both too long and I didn't care, I looked like a clown. My father was sitting at a back table. He was drinking a glass of wine and picking at a salad. You look well, he said to me, when I sat down. Not really, I said, not really, I don't, and I smiled faintly. Soon, my boots would be spilling dirty snow all over the tiled floor, and someone would be mopping around me. I smoothed my hands over Wes's white shirt, felt for the safety pin I'd used to bind the spot where a button had gone missing. I wore no makeup. My face was bare and tired-looking despite the fact that all I did was sleep, I did everything from bed, I didn't really sleep, I lay there and when I did drop off, I had bad dreams, my days and nights were reversed. It felt like the middle of the night sitting there across from Paul, like it was strange that we were together, there was something indecent about it, something artificial about being with Paul in that restaurant. It was like we were in an airport lounge. I thought of Juliet's description of jet lag, and sitting across from my father, I too felt that my soul was trying to catch up with my body. I had seen Paul only twice this past year. We'd met briefly in the park close to my apartment. Under trees that were furred with moss and bowed together, we'd sat on a bench and had a shallow conversation. We had been in touch here and there, most intensely after I had lost my pregnancy, when I would call Paul at night from under my bedcovers and I would speak to Paul in an unguarded way, when I could hear the rushed hard whisper of my voice, issued directly from my gut. I couldn't talk to Wes in that way because Wes was already too worried about me and my state of mind, and I knew that

Paul wouldn't be. Once we hung up, he would go on with his life, with the things that mattered to him, and while I knew that I mattered to Paul, and he saw that I was in a crisis state, I was his daughter, I was like a passing phenomenon, like a sunset, I would rise and I would fall and there wasn't much he could do about it. Paul ordered his main course. I ordered French fries and mayonnaise. Don't you want anything else? Paul asked. No, I said. Paul's eyes were overly bright, that beautiful, concentrated green. He was a beautiful man, he was unbothered, he looked well, he looked well taken care of, he looked rich. Leaving us for Cherry had been a tactical move. Paul hadn't responded to my angry birthday email. I hadn't expected him to, he typically ducked from any confrontation. And yet alone in my apartment, hour after hour, I checked my inbox, I checked it to see if Paul had responded, if Juliet had responded, I'd copied her on the email. Then I checked my folders to be sure I'd sent the angry email to Paul, it had been such a relief to write it, I confirmed that I had sent it, and then I felt nauseated with guilt. What if something had happened to Paul on the island, what if he slipped and bashed his head on the rocks, what if he hit a shoal on his way back to the mainland and was thrown from the boat into that endless water, what if he died in his sleep and those words were my final words to him? I emailed Juliet to ask if I'd been too harsh with Paul and whether I was out of my mind, and I said, Tell me the truth, don't hold back, and she said No, no, not at all, what I had written was fair and reasonable. She thought Eva's silence through my loss was unconscionable, it only proved Eva was a sociopath like her mother, and then Juliet wrote that, for all intents and purposes, Eva was dead to her, but before burying Eva in her mind, Juliet was placing a curse on Eva, the curse of a life without love, real love. And then Juliet wrote, But seriously, Mona, are you alright?

Eva is getting married—Paul was sitting across from me and talking in the nice restaurant. The restaurant was almost empty. We were there at a weird hour, too early for dinner, too late for lunch. The candles were not lit. I got cold after my fast walk through the thick snow. The server brought me my heavy coat and so I was sitting there in my snow boots and my heavy coat across from Paul, my hair, I was sure, was some wet tangle, my face bloated and dead-looking with sadness. Through the windows, I could see the snow continuing to fall and accumulate. I imagined the walk back to my apartment, the early dusk, that granular light that comforted me because it meant the day was disintegrating, the time when I was supposed to participate in society, the time when I was supposed to get things done was nearing its end. The climb up those stairs to our fourth-floor apartment. I hoped I wouldn't see a neighbour or anyone I knew, but then no one seemed to fully recognize me. They always said my name as a question. Mona? Paul had ordered a glass of red wine for me. I hadn't noticed. I thanked Paul and took a deep drink of the wine. It spread through my throat, I felt it float up into my head, I felt it behind my face, inside the thin bones that held my brain and my eyes. A decent guy—Paul was describing Eva's fiancé. He's a medical student, an internist, he's Swedish. I'm not sure why you are telling me this, I said to Paul. And Paul hesitated and said, Well, I have no one to talk to, I mean, really talk to, and his eyes flitted nervously over the almost empty restaurant. Then Paul told me that the wedding would take place that coming summer. It would be on the island. As I probably expected, Juliet and I wouldn't be invited. And then Paul cleared his throat and said there would be some kind of reception at his and Cherry's house that fall, after the wedding, and Juliet and I would be invited to that reception. Paul said the reception had been his idea and he considered it a test of Eva's loyalty. Paul's brow creased, he shifted in his seat. He knew as well as I did. In the family, it was not Paul but Eva who designed the tests of loyalty. I told Paul that I wouldn't be going to any reception for Eva. As you probably expected—I used Paul's phrasing against him and took on his cadence and physicality—I won't be going to any reception for Eva. Paul switched tracks. He had a problem, he told me. He didn't know what to do about Judd. Judd was his closest friend, he wanted Judd at Eva's wedding, but Judd was married to Natasha now, and Paul couldn't even say Natasha's name without Cherry going into a spiteful rant. Cherry hated Natasha. Eva hated everyone. And there were no grounds for their hate, it felt pulled from the air. The whole thing is a mess, Paul said, and he drained his wine, lifted his hand, the server appeared and poured more. My glass had been emptied too, was filled. I drank. The wine cushioned every-thing. I sat there in my heavy winter coat and waited for Paul to keep speaking. I still felt cold, but I wasn't sure what to do about it. I looked around, it was winter. It was winter in the restaurant. My jaw was tight, my body was tight, the light was blue, my legs shook, I felt only my bones, protrud-ing outward, uncovered. I've been writing, Paul said. That's good, I replied. I already knew that Paul was writing. Natasha had told me about his finished manuscript, his fourth un-published book since *Daughter* if my count was correct. Paul leaned forward, he put his hand on the table like he was reaching for my hand, but I looked down at my hand and couldn't lift it, my hand was limp and upturned and pale like a fish stranded on my leg, on Wes's black pants. It lay there, an abstract thing. What is it? Paul was saying. Is it Eva? Is it the wedding? You're crying, Mona. Sorry, I said, I don't mean to. I used Wes's long shirtsleeve to wipe my face. I'll be fine, I said. It's not Eva. It's not the wedding. And I heard myself laugh. I drank down the wine, but now it was like rot in my throat, sour, and I asked Paul, What do you want? Why did you want to see me? And Paul's face looked injured. His lips parted as if for air, his teeth were grey from the wine, I could see his eyes searching for my sympathy, for a way in, and he said, Last night, Cherry and I got into a bad fight. Paul described coming home from the shooting range to a dark house, he called out Cherry's name and was met with silence. Paul assumed she must be out. He went upstairs to his study, and found Cherry sitting at his desk with her back to him like a spectre, her presence startled him. Jesus, Paul said, replaying that moment for me, the moment he found Cherry sitting there in the darkest dark of his study. Cherry was so still Paul thought she'd had a heart attack or some kind of fatal incident, she was that still. Paul flicked on the light and said Cherry's name again, and this time she spun his desk chair around to face him. In her hands was Paul's latest manuscript. Paul had hidden it from Cherry. Cherry had decimated his work for most of their relationship and he was catching up to this fact. He'd convinced himself that Cherry was protecting him from his downfall, when now he realized she was playing on his self-doubt, raking through his self-hatred. Cherry read Paul's work to minimize him, her eyes were scopes. He was mimetic, a hack. His talent was built on the talent of others. Cherry's criticism was as precise and punishing as Paul's own inner voice. It was like a photonegative, eerie and accurate. She wanted Paul for herself, Paul knew this—for Cherry, love was ownership—she wanted to be the only one to have access to his thoughts, and yet every ugly word, everything she said, Paul felt in his lowest moments to be true. Anyway, she must have really dug, Paul said, to find the manuscript, I'd buried it. Paul confronted Cherry about entering his study, and rifling through his drawers. Paul said he could hear himself, his voice was raised, he was yelling. Cherry never yelled, she did the opposite, she whispered so he was always forced to move closer to her. Cherry called Paul's point about entering his study a secondary one, it was a minor point, and then she said his thinking was petty and small. The real trespass, Cherry said, is this, and she shook Paul's work at him. All over the manuscript was Natasha's handwriting. Not just edits, Paul specified to me in the restaurant, but additions. Well, not just additions, but entire scenes, entire chapters. Natasha had written entire chapters, Mona, and they were great. They were so great, and here Paul nearly met my eyes, just like they were for *Daughter*.

Paul said, I don't know who I am when I am inside that house, and he sat there looking helpless. I could tell that Paul had more to tell me. What do you want? Why did you want to see me? I asked Paul again, and he said, I'm sorry, I'm a bit drunk from the wine. I got my manuscript to safety, Paul told me. I have the novel on my laptop of course and a hard drive, but it doesn't have any of Natasha's contributions. On the way here to meet you, I dropped the manuscript off at my assistant's, well, at my friend's. And then Paul inhaled, and I watched his lungs fill under his blue sweater, his eyes drift and soften, and I knew what was coming and Paul said, I'm in love. I'm just so in love. And Paul looked down to the tiled floor, to the grey pool of melted snow around my boots, soaking the hem of my heavy coat, and he said, I don't want to drag you into my mess the way I did the last time. Then Paul rubbed at his features, which were also my features, he rubbed at them as if to erase them, and he said, Now, you, Mona. You. What are you up to? And I answered Paul, and I told him the truth which was, Nothing.

.   .   .

When I got home that evening, after my encounter with Paul, I crawled under the bedcovers. Wes was out, I could smell the winter on my skin, I could not get warm. I stripped off Wes's damp clothes and lowered my body into the bath, steam filled the room and made it tropical. I remembered smoking in the bathtub when I was twelve, my mother sitting on the closed toilet seat beside me after our steak dinner, she had her red lipstick on, red lipstick, my mother said, raises a face from the dead, my mother passed me the lit cigarette with the red imprint of her mouth on the filter. I climbed out of the bath in my empty apartment. The steam dispersed. I dried my skin, touching my skin still hurt, I should have an eight-month-old son, I put on my thickest things, I put on my heavy overcoat, I could not get warm. I walked the rooms of my apartment and they looked like someone else's rooms. They were the rooms of my former self, her small concerns, she knew nothing. Wes texted to say he was going to be late, the shoot had been delayed, he would be stuck on set for hours still, and I wondered if Wes was having an affair, maybe with his co-star, or maybe Wes was having an affair with Ani, maybe Ani had been his true love all along and what had happened with me was an aberration. The stillbirth only proved that Wes being with me was an aberration. I deserved the stillbirth because I'd gotten together with Wes after he had been in a relationship with Ani. No good woman did that to her closest friend. It was a code and I had broken the code. It was Ani who should be with Wes, it was Ani who should be the mother, not me. They should have the life together. It was so clear. My still-birth happened because I'd had an abortion at fifteen, because I had let myself be raped, because I had stolen my closest friend's true love. My phone was ringing. On my bedside table was a loose polaroid of me and Wes together, we were kissing, we were in a dark bar, I had to stand on my toes to kiss Wes, Wes was in his parka and he had pulled me into his parka to kiss my mouth. To kiss Wes was to go underwater. I held the glossy photo. I thought of our life, our aliveness, as a combined force. After the stillbirth, I handed my aliveness to Wes. I gave Wes my aliveness. I had no use for my aliveness. The day followed the night followed the day and I could hardly get through that cycle. My phone was ringing. I saw my reflection in the tall front window of our living room and I was a woman in a heavy overcoat with my arms out, fumbling. I looked down. My feet were bare. My hair was wet. It hung to my waist now. I could hear it drip on the hardwood floor. My phone was ringing. Wes's talent was to fake life. It was to call up emotions in himself and to perform those emotions. Wes's talent was to make words written by other people sound like his own words, to make invented selves appear real. Maybe Wes had been performing his emotions on me, the words he had been speaking were leached from scripts, the selves I thought I knew were not Wes. Never Wes. I didn't know Wes because Wes was an assembly of parts. Wes did not exist. Our son did not exist. I remembered the sleeping pills in the bathroom cabinet. I made a calculation. I calculated what it might be to exit the cycle, to skip the daylight, to enter the ongoing night. Night would not touch my back the way my mother did. Night would not heaven and hell me the way my father did. Night would not shame me the way Wes did. Wes with his beauty and his motor. Wes who was anyone and no one. My mother had described it as stepping off. I can't lie to you, my mother had said to me that night in the bathroom when she described briefly losing her life. And I know I am being reckless, I am out of control, my mother had said, you are not even a teenager, you haven't even gotten your period, but I can't lie to you. It's not as if darkness has no feel to it. It does. It held me and it asked for nothing in return. In my empty apartment, I went to the bathroom. And my phone dinged. This time, it was Ani's name on the screen, and I thought to myself, they are coordinating. Wes and Ani are in Ani's coach house with candles burning and something on the stovetop, and they are coordinating because they don't want to hurt me, they know they can't tell me yet. I can't handle it. I'm too sick and hopeless, I'm too sad. Ani and Wes are waiting for me to feel better before they tell me that they are the rightful union, they had been the rightful union all along. They are having the life together. I was the aberration. Ani was pregnant with Wes's child, that was why I had not seen Ani, because Ani could not lie to my face. Nature had proven I was the aberration, nature couldn't survive in my body, Wes's child couldn't survive in my body. And now I pulled the sleeping pills from the cabinet, twisting the cap. I opened Ani's message, how would she lie, how would she cover up the affair with Wes, her true love, and Ani said she was writing from the airport in Athens. Ani was in Greece, I'd forgotten. She had received a prestigious grant and was apprenticing with a carpenter in Greece. The carpenter built elaborate stages. Ani had been building elaborate stages with a master carpenter in Greece. Ani was texting from the Athens airport: *Flying soon. There is a Greek word that means both always and everything, and the word is Panda. More in person. Panda.* And then I heard the front door open, and it was Wes saying my name, Wes in the bathroom, he had his long arms around me, I could feel his heart pounding through his chest, and he was saying, I didn't hear from you, Mona. I have to hear from you. I have to hear from you. What is happening here? And Wes was shaking the sleeping pills into the toilet bowl, he was throwing the empty pill bottle across the small room, he was holding my face in his warm hands.

FOUR

It was the first good dream I had had in so long. I was in a large bed, the covers were dark and filmy, and beside me in the large bed under the dark and filmy covers was a deer. The deer had a feminine face, she had a beautiful structure to her face, she looked like Meryl Streep, she had outer-space eyes that were wet and brown, they were shimmering with the light that pricked through the covers in silver-white needles, she was seducing me, I stroked her coat, her coat was velvet under my touch, the deer had a male sex part, and I was having sex with the deer. I was telling the psychiatrist about my dream. I felt embarrassed talking about sex with the psychiatrist so I addressed her feet, her scuffed leather slippers side by side, against the patterned carpet. Eventually, I looked up at the psychiatrist's face. She was nearly expressionless, but I felt her attention on me steady and bright like a lamp. Outside, tree branches thrashed in the wind and rain pelted her office windows. It was a spring storm. I would walk home, and be obscured by the weather. I was still thinking in this way, how to hide myself in the daylight. But the thing about the dream, I was telling my psychiatrist inside her office, and I'm not saying that I'm beautiful, and I'm not saying that I'm Meryl Streep, the thing about the dream is that the dream deer was me. I was having sex with myself. I was with myself. I was forgiving myself. I had been seeing the psychiatrist for four months, since that January night Wes found me soaking wet in my overcoat in our bathroom with an open bottle of sleeping pills in my hand. The sessions were forty-five minutes long. They were two afternoons a week. The psychiatrist's office was like a junk shop crowded with furniture and plants, tables and paintings. When I first entered her office, the psychiatrist said, Sit wherever you like. It took me a while to decide on a navy-blue armchair. I sat in the big armchair and felt my body get tossed by the sea, I heaved and cried, and the psychiatrist sat directly across from me, my lamp. There was a washroom on the same floor with three stalls. After my sessions with the psychiatrist, I would walk to the washroom and pray it was empty so I could splash cold water on my face. If it wasn't empty, I wouldn't use it, I would turn around. I wore an army coat with a large hood. I walked to the office and home, two hours total. My psychiatric treatment was my occupation. I was never late for my psychiatrist.

Her office was in a low-level white building in a wealthier part of the city just off a busy commercial street that was lined with upscale food shops. It was close to Paul and Cherry's house. What if I walked by Cherry with her shopping bags? What if I walked by Eva? Her semester was over, she was planning her island wedding, she could be here in the city. In my mind, I had encountered Eva a thousand times. On the closing night of my play, *Margot*, I thought I saw Eva in one of the back rows of the theatre. I knew her posture as well as my own, the muscular set of her shoulders, she was a rower, her chest was broad as a shield, her hair was pulled into a ponytail, when Eva pulled her hair into a ponytail she looked troubled by her hair, she scolded her hair into place. My body flooded with energy when I thought I was looking at Eva from the stage, I felt electrocuted under those hot lights, looking at Eva in the audience, touching the thin gold chain at her neck, challenging me with her competitive eyes. Leaving my psychiatrist's office after describing sex with the dream deer, I wondered what Eva would do if she passed me on the sidewalk of that commercial street. Cradling flowers in her arms, holding her dry cleaning like a dead body. Would Eva glare at me? Would she spit? When I encountered Eva in my mind, she forgot all about the estrangement, she forgot to ignore me. She rushed toward me only to do an about-face when she remembered her pact with herself to cut contact, her pact with her mother, I was a cheat and a parasite, I was not good, I was not trustworthy, I had betrayed Eva, my younger sister, my fragile sister, all for the moving target of our father's love.

I did see Cherry once along that busy commercial street. She was walking toward me in exercise clothes. I had not seen Cherry since Wes and I had gone up to the island for that one night. I slowed to a stop. Cherry rushed past me. We were enemies. I had never had an enemy before. What would I have said to Cherry had she stopped? Would that be the last time I saw Cherry? In her exercise clothes walking that busy commercial street? Should I have given her a diaper? Should I have sprayed her with a hose? Cherry was my enemy, Eva was my enemy, Paul lived with my enemies. Paul would have withdrawn from Cherry by now. She had gone too far when she rummaged through his desk. Paul would have had a lock installed on his study door. Cherry would be on the offensive. She had lost control of Paul and she needed to regain it. She was exercising, she was thinking about her figure, she was thinking about her grim future as a single woman in her sixties, she was thinking about Eva's wedding. She needed to keep Paul, she needed to keep her life intact. Meanwhile, Paul would say he was going to the shooting range and he would drive his car out to a semi-basement apartment in the suburbs filled with books. Paul would see Sigrid whenever he could. I felt Cherry and Paul would soon implode. They were the enemies. The daughters were just following their lead.

· · ·

Eva's wedding would be at the end of July, her wedding was one month away. Paul wrote to me and Juliet from the island. He was commuting between the island and the city and he was miserable. He had installed a cot in his writing studio. He slept with his shotgun in his hands. The geese were frantic. The geese sounded the way Paul felt, Paul had stopped shooting the geese, he absorbed their anxiety, he let the geese shit wherever they wanted, the island was covered in shit. He had gone off his meds. He had barricaded his door. When he was in his writing studio on the island, Paul wrote, he barricaded his door with his desk. Eva and Cherry spent their days in the main house plotting the end of him. Eva swam around the island like a shark while Cherry timed her sleek body. Cherry had a stopwatch. Eva was a killing machine. Cherry had an industrial broom and she scrubbed the green geese shit off the rocks. Paul was the geese. Their shit was in damp tubes and it was the colour of Paul's eyes. Cherry spent her nights in her headlamp cleaning the rocks, blinding Paul. Cherry wanted the shotgun, that was why Paul slept with it. Paul was sick, he wrote to me and Juliet, that his daughters were not going to be part of an event that would gather his closest friends. Paul wanted to jettison Eva's wedding, but, Paul wrote, he only had so much fight in him. He was conserving his energy for the larger battle. Paul was not inviting Judd to Eva's wedding because Cherry hated Natasha. Natasha had made it clear to Paul that had she been invited to the wedding, she would not have attended. She didn't drink with the devil, she didn't raise a glass to her daughters' tormenter, she called Cherry *Chernobyl*, she said Cherry left only carnage in her wake. Judd could care less about Eva's wedding. Judd was a happy man. He had Paul's latest manuscript in his hands, and he deemed it fucking good, fucking worthy, it was big game, it was the next *Daughter*. Judd and his hellhound, Hunk, sitting in their sedan, could smell money, Paul wrote. But it was never enough. Now Judd was leaning on Paul for his previous three manuscripts to determine how to release them, in what order, how best to announce Paul Dean's triumphant return to the world of letters. Paul didn't even know if he had a key to the storage locker. His three manuscripts were in that storage locker. That was Cherry's department. Cherry had the key. Paul wrote that when he was in his writing studio, he was not writing, he was looking at images of the plastic islands in the ocean, Styrofoam and plastic congregating and binding into these monstrous formations that killed everything, these murderous formations in the water, the life-giving water, and he felt he had been snared by one of these Styrofoam islands. He was stuck, he was running out of air, he was dying. That is an ugly thing to write, but that is how I feel, and you are the only ones I can be truthful with. In a couple of days, I drive down to the city, Paul wrote. I'll make the four-hour drive. I'll have the house to myself. I'll look for the key to the storage locker. The thing about those three manuscripts, Paul confided in his email, was that Natasha had not read them. Natasha had not added to the manuscripts. What Judd loved was Natasha. What Judd loved was Natasha's writing. Maybe Cherry had cancelled the storage locker, and the contents had gone to charity. Maybe the manuscripts had been destroyed. They were handwritten. They were written before I had an assistant, before I had Sigrid. And then Paul wrote to me and Juliet,

I'm in love, I'm just so in love. I picture what it might be like to be free.

Juliet responded to Paul. You have some love in your life. Good for you. But, Juliet warned, your timing with Sigrid could not be much worse. Eva's wedding was fast approaching. Paul needed to play his part for another month. One month was hardly a lifetime. One month was not a life sentence. Eva would find out about Sigrid soon enough. It was not worth outing the affair just because Paul was impatient with his circumstances. His circumstances were of his own making. Like all of us, Paul had built his own life, including his confinement. He had built his Styrofoam island. You must take the long view. Or, at the very least, the longer view. You are tempting fate. You are running in a dangerous environment. These people do not fight the way we do, Juliet cautioned. Cherry would have Paul followed, she would involve her sons who would track Paul, she would dig up dirt on Paul, she would sully his reputation and destroy his career. Did Paul have a plan in place if he separated from Cherry? Did Paul have a will? Paul needed to recover the three manuscripts from the storage locker, and get them to Judd and Natasha. Juliet did not want to overthink Natasha's role in Paul's success, this was not the time, but it did not sit well with Juliet that Natasha had never been credited or compensated for her part in *Daughter*, that she had been working the front desk of a radio station for the last twenty years while Paul enriched himself off translation and film deals, residuals from adverts for Scotch and cigars. What was Paul going to do about that? Juliet wrote that she was okay with Sigrid, she was okay with the fact that Sigrid was her age, Paul was starved for love, she got it, but it was crazy in her mind that he was pursuing this other relationship when there was so much at stake. Juliet told Paul he needed to get his priorities straight. He needed to get back on his meds. He needed to play father of the bride. He needed to ice Sigrid for the time being. Sorry, Juliet wrote, but you need a swift kick in the ass.

Paul did not respond to Juliet other than to say that, in his paranoia, he had overstated Natasha's contribution to his work, we could ask Natasha ourselves, she would agree, his work was his legacy, he had little else to show for his life, he had always wanted to be a man who mattered and it was his work that made him matter. He alone was the author of *Daughter*.

I did not respond. Juliet emailed me separately. She felt guilty, she had been trying to help Paul, her intention had been to help, but she reread her email and she'd been too harsh. Paul's life with Cherry and Eva must be so lonely, she hated to isolate Paul more than he already was. He was vulnerable. He was confused. She had been out of line. She could apologize, offer some warmth. Still, Juliet concluded, Paul did need a wake-up call.

I agreed with Juliet. I parroted Juliet, and wrote that yes, Paul did need a wake-up call. Then I told Juliet she had nothing to feel guilty for. It was our conditioning to feel badly when we called Paul out on his behaviour. We'd been indoctrinated to protect Paul when he never protected us in turn. I didn't understand how that sleight of hand had happened, but it had. In her email, Juliet had done Paul a favour. She had rejigged his thinking. For the moment, he was being resistant, but soon enough, he would see her logic. He would come around. The last thing Paul could afford was to get caught.

.　.　.

It was the following day, the day after Paul defended his legacy to me and Juliet, that Paul called Sigrid from the northwestern end of the island. He had to cover his left ear with his hand to hear Sigrid. Nearby, a bulldozer cleared an area of brush. Eva had decided she would perform her marriage vows on the spot where Paul stood, on that flat expanse of rock, where the sun would set the July night of her wedding. Just south of that photogenic spot, a party tent would be erected to accommodate the guests. Paul was concerned about the placement of the party tent. The winds were highest on that side of the island, the party tent could collapse on the guests. Cherry told Paul the technology was more advanced now, Cherry snapped that the party tent would be fine, the party tent could withstand even the highest winds. Close to where Paul stood with his phone, the bulldozer lurched forward and back, flattening all that grew from the ground. Two brothers from the mainland shuttled the scrub and brush to the barge that was secured to the dock, the brothers were shaped like bulls, the barge was tied opposite Paul and Cherry's speedboat, *Evangeline*. Paul looked at the barge. In a month, that same barge would bring the guests to the island for the wedding, the guests that did not include his best friend or his daughters, Mona and Juliet. Paul looked out at the open water. Over the phone, Paul told Sigrid he didn't know how much longer he could do this. Being without her was hell. He wanted to make a life with her. He was at a total loss. He had emailed his daughters, and rather than offering their support, the eldest, Juliet, had torn into him, she was so conservative, and the younger, Mona, had not even responded. He had seen Mona through her darkest nights, and she had not even responded, Paul repeated this slight to Sigrid in a hurt voice. For Sigrid, Paul's voice was an insemination, his voice filled her body, it entered her bloodstream and her cells. She wanted him, and she told him so. Paul muttered seductive things back to Sigrid, but it was tiresome, he felt teleprompted, he had said these same things before to Lee. Maybe Sigrid was a passing infatuation and nothing more. What if he never saw her again? Would he be alright? He would be alright. This disturbed Paul. He did not debase himself, he needed to debase himself. Natasha did that. She faced death because of love. She went low and then lower because of love. And her sentences were better than his. Paul was a decent writer, but he was not a great one. Judd was wrong about Paul. Judd was old, he didn't know the culture. Paul wasn't relevant anymore. No one wanted to hear from a sulking playboy, an ex-boxer long past his prime who had constant pain in his jaw and his chest. Paul looked down at the cavity where part of his rib was missing. Sigrid loved that cavity. She projected the Bible story on to that cavity, and it bugged Paul when she did that, he felt responsible for her creation. Why did women have to be so intense? It was their fault he felt like an imposter. It was their fault he felt like a false god. Just then, the bulldozer crept too close to Paul's boots, and Paul twisted around. He lifted his arms in exasperation, and charged at the operator. Paul saw himself in the windshield, and he looked like the geese in midflight, he looked frantic and pointless, he had spent his life chasing love when he did not even know what love was.

Paul got off the call with Sigrid. He would see her soon enough. He made promises that would be impossible to keep. He had to go or Cherry might suspect something. He would see Sigrid in the city in the next couple of days. He had to go. Paul slipped his phone into his jacket pocket and walked toward the main house. Inside, Cherry and Eva were sitting at the long dining table in their sweaters. The sweaters were similar, though not identical. Eva's was a paler blue and cable-knit. They were drinking black tea and eating wedges of pink grapefruit. Eva was consuming very little these days, she had plastic wrap wound around her waist and thighs. By way of explanation, she had told Paul she needed to go down a dress size. Paul nodded approvingly at his daughter, but had no idea what she was talking about. Paul entered the main house. Upon seeing Paul, Cherry and Eva both felt for the thin gold chains at their necks, Paul had bought the chains after the horror show with Lee. Had Lee been real? She felt real. Was Sigrid real? Paul didn't know yet. Despite the wind and cold, Paul announced to Cherry and Eva that he was going for a swim. He'd had a tense conversation with Judd, he lied, and he needed to clear his head, he needed the shock of the ocean. Paul was keyed up. In his haste, he left his quilted flannel jacket folded over the back of the couch. His secret phone, the phone he used with Sigrid, was still in the breast pocket.

Through the glass, Cherry and Eva watched Paul's hurried movements as he made his way down to the water, down to the new beach, out of view of the workers. It was hard going. A firm crust had formed on the imported sand so every time Paul took a step, he broke through the crust and had to pull himself from a crater. The dunes had been a disappointment. Sand was in everything. When Cherry swallowed, she swallowed sand. Cherry and Eva watched as Paul stripped off his clothes and dropped his towel. He had a formidable body. Block-shaped and sturdy like a gladiator. All of his injuries were on the surface, his skewed jaw, his sunken chest. They could see the fog of Paul's breath. The sky was slate grey, a pitiless grey, the grey of a headstone, and with the light blocked, so was the water. Paul rubbed his arms roughly, he stood at the shoreline, then ran at the forceful currents, doing a shallow dive into the ocean. Late June, and after an unseasonable cold snap, the water was just sixty degrees, it could stop his heart. Cherry and Eva watched the big splash as Paul's body hit the water. Soon, Paul surfaced, and he let out a cry that was happiness and pain mixed together. Typical Paul. He was so overblown. Eva and Cherry went back to what they were doing. Eva was planning to wear a crown of flowers on her wedding day. She and Cherry were finalizing the flowers. Eva didn't want the floral crown to be too ornate. It was already a crown. The flowers they were considering were flamboyant to her eye, she wanted less flamboyant flowers. The flowers were tacky. She wanted more subtle flowers. The flowers were too expressive, too needy, too keen to be loved. The flowers were like actresses. They were like Mona with her innocent, wide eyes, her grainy voice, the way she moved her body like it was for sale, casing the room to see what she could steal from it. Mona pretended

to be shy and deferent, she pretended to be quietly observant, this sentient artist at the edge of the world, when all
she wanted was to gorge on everyone's hearts and minds.
Tragedia. Mona stood there like the injured child in the rain.
And Mona always got what she wanted. Her pain was her
subterfuge. There was something embarrassing about the
flowers, something repellent. Had Mona worn a crown of
flowers when she played Ophelia? She had. That was it. Eva
had watched Mona's final performance. She had to admit
Mona was good as Ophelia, she was unnerving actually, even
though Eva hated that role, it was so weak to kill yourself
as a result of not getting what you wanted. Suicide was a
tantrum gone fatal. Whatever. Mona hardly figured into it,
Eva had not seen her in two, almost three, years. She was
relieved by not seeing Mona. Mona was the physical re-
minder that Eva was less loved by Paul, she was the inferior
daughter, and Eva could feel Cherry compensate for Paul's
deficit, as if between Paul and Cherry there was a scale, and
Cherry had to forever check and correct the balance of
love for Eva. Eva felt her eyes fill. The room appeared half-
submerged. A tear dropped into her black tea. She watched
the ripple made by the tear, then dried her eyes with the cuff
of her sweater. Eva did an exercise program online, it was a
military-style workout, and between moves, when you had
to reset your body, the teacher would say, Organize yourself.
Organize yourself. Eva pushed Mona from her mind, and re-
trained her focus on the task at hand. The floral crown had

been Cherry's idea. Eva was not sure the floral crown was her style. She was not a sentimental person. But, she wanted to please Cherry. Cherry had done so much for her, and asked for so little in return. Whenever Eva called Cherry with a problem, whatever the hour, Cherry answered. Of Cherry's children, Eva knew she was the most loved by their mother, and this love was a natural love, not just the counterweight to Paul's insufficient love. Eva liked looking down at her brothers from the top rung, they were limited, she liked knowing that the last image in her mother's mind at night was her, not them. She would never slip from her position. She would do anything for Cherry. Cherry needed her protection. Despite Cherry's poise, Eva could still sense her mother's hurt after Paul's affair with Lee. Cherry moved like she was concealing an injury. Cherry never spoke about it, she would perform her life until it felt real again, but Eva saw the effort in her mother, the strain of bending reality to her will. From behind the glass, Eva watched the source of her mother's pain. Paul exited the ocean, staggering onto the shore. Even in nature, he was vain. He shook the salt water from his hair and his eardrums, wrapped the towel around his wide, straight waist. He huffed steam, stepping along the sand path, collecting his trail of clothes, rushing to the outdoor shower, his lips turning a pretty violet. Paul had humiliated her mother, and Eva would never forgive him. Eva would wear the crown. And she would agree to her mother's flower selection, however romantic. Scrolling through white flowers together in the main house, Cherry and Eva heard a buzzing sound. Eva stayed at the long dining table. Cherry located the buzzing sound. She pulled Paul's secret phone from his breast pocket. She held it in her hands, delicately like a nest. She read Sigrid's name. She knew Judd had hired an assistant for Paul. Then Cherry read Sigrid's desperate message to Paul. Then she read the stream of desperate messages between Sigrid and Paul.

.   .   .

I was sitting in the navy-blue armchair across from my psychiatrist when my phone buzzed. I'd forgotten to shut it down before my session. Without looking at the screen, I shut down my phone. Sorry, I said to my psychiatrist. It was a cool summer afternoon, I felt nauseated. There was a new smell in her office, it was an animal-feed smell. I sat upright in my army coat and relayed the exchange between Paul and Juliet. When I was done, my psychiatrist asked, And what does Paul tell Cherry, what does Paul tell Eva? I considered her question. I saw where she was going with her question. I told my psychiatrist it was not so simple. Paul was steered by his urges, he was impulsive, insecure, self-obsessed, but he was not a mastermind. He was too sloppy to be a mastermind. I defended Paul. I recounted our period of extreme closeness when Paul was with Lee. I was forced to admit that when their relationship ended, I was kicked to the dirt. But, it was not so simple, I said again to my psychiatrist. After my stillbirth, the only person I could talk to in the way that I needed to talk was Paul. I could not even talk to Wes, to Ani, Natasha, or Juliet. I could only talk to Paul. Paul listened to me.

But did he? my psychiatrist asked.

.   .   .

Ani says that when a white man is described as a genius, even once, he can get away with anything including murder. I mean in terms of examples where do I even start, Ani said.

.   .   .

During that bad winter, if Wes was out of the apartment, and I was lying in bed, staring up at the ceiling, the water stain in the corner spreading and changing like the Milky Way, like a virus in the body, I would search Magnus's name on the internet. Ani's theory about the internet was that in our agnostic society, we were left with a void, we needed a god to tell us what was good, whether we were worthy, whether we were liked, and so we made the internet our god. Ani's theory was that there must be a place inside of us where we want to feel badly. Ani's theory was that most internet searches were a form of self-harm. *Magnus Beck.* Magnus was photographed running in LA. He was wearing headphones, tights under his shorts, he was shirtless, his skin lung-pink under the LA sun. Magnus was in jeans and bare feet, pulling his garbage can to the curb, giving the paparazzi a dead-eyed look. Art Basel and Magnus was leaving a Miami nightclub with two models and an unnamed friend. Magnus was back in LA at a service station filling his Ardennes Green 1991 Range Rover Classic. He was walking his rescue, a light-grey pit bull called Anaïs Nin. *Magnus Beck*. Magnus won't give interviews, Magnus won't speak to the press because his films speak to the press, there was nothing more to say, he was not a show pony. Magnus was the Troubled Fantasist. Magnus was the new Stanley Kubrick. *Magnus Beck*. Magnus and his married lead actress were in the front seat of his black Porsche 996. Flashbulbs lit up Magnus's windshield, the lead actress buried her face in her hands. Magnus and the lead actress were wheeling suitcases through the Cape Town airport. Magnus and the lead actress shared a passionate kiss on an Italian balcony, her back was bent over the railing, it was evening, they were dressed up, they both had lit cigarettes in their hands, they held the lit cigarettes away from each other. *Magnus Beck*. Magnus in jeans and bare feet and the lead actress in a white string bikini fighting by a private pool in Croatia. Magnus throwing a lounge chair at the lead actress who said later they were just rehearsing a scene, Magnus's genius was that he did as much as he could in the wild. *Magnus Beck*. Nominated for the Best Director and Best Picture Oscars, Magnus was straight-faced on the red carpet in a classic tuxedo, his mother as his date in an ornate dress, she was beside him, standing there, not quite touching. Magnus was lying low in New York with a coffee cup in his hand, sunglasses on, his phone to his ear. The Oscar winner was nearly unrecognizable now with his unruly beard. *Magnus Beck*. Magnus with his arm cinched possessively around a young woman's bony shoulder. They were walking Anaïs Nin through Greenwich Village. The young woman was underdressed, sun-starved, leggy and aloof like an indoor cat. She gave the paparazzi a heavy-lidded, quizzical look. No one knew much about the young woman other than that, after a secret ceremony officiated by David Lynch in a baroque hunting lodge, she was now Magnus Beck's wife.

.　.　.

When *Daughter* was published, Paul wrote a companion piece for *Playboy* called "The Lower Chambers of My Heart." In the *Playboy* piece, Paul looked back on the January night when a section of his rib was cut from his thirty-eight-year-old chest, and grafted to his jaw after his jaw was splintered by a right hook. He stood to win a hundred bucks in that Las Vegas fight, he needed the hundred bucks to get home, his second daughter was about to get born. After the *Playboy* piece came out, *Daughter* became a bestseller, and young writers visited Paul, drank with Paul, and asked Paul if they could see his scars. They felt jealous of his injury, his injury was as famous as he was. After readings of *Daughter*, fans would crowd around Paul, mostly women, and Paul would list the things that fit most nicely in his cavity: a tongue, a small breast, a cigar, a set of keys, a baby's foot, a champagne flute, the muzzle of a shotgun. When he pressed the muzzle of his shotgun into his cavity, Paul would say to the swell of women, he could get the muzzle right against the lower chambers of his heart.

In the photo that accompanied Paul's piece in *Playboy*, Paul had a cigar in his mouth despite his heavily bandaged jaw, and in his muscled forearms, a baby in her christening gown. The baby was me, Mona, named for the Las Vegas nurse Paul credited with saving his ability to talk and smoke and kiss the night I was born.

.   .   .

After the session with my psychiatrist, when she asked, And what does Paul tell Cherry, tell Eva, I went to the washroom. The washroom door whined when I pushed it open. I crouched down to the polished floor to peer beneath the stalls, the washroom was empty. I felt around in my coat pocket for the stick wrapped in its stiff plastic, the pregnancy test. My phone was off. I stood before the wide mirror. I ran the tap and made the water ice cold and pressed my hands into my face. My hands were shutters, I opened and closed them. I looked at myself in the wide mirror of the empty washroom of that low-level white building. I looked like a regular person, but a bit off, there was something a bit off about this regular person. Her eyes were dark like stones, they were dull, and then they were mad, wet, shifting. My hair was to my tailbone now, I raked my fingers through my scalp and caught long strands, I balled them between my palms, and tried to drain the clusters of hair down the sink. They would not drain, they sat there in the bowl of the sink like small animals. I did not have wisdom, I did not have resourcefulness. I did not have these good, calm and useful attributes, I'd told my psychiatrist. But, I had new insight. I had new insight and it ran through me like a current and to convert the surfeit of energy I felt, I was writing again. I wrote as an act of conversion, of taking the severed parts of my life and assembling them, and in assembling them into a new form, separate from me, they lost their power over me. I had not written for a year and a half. Wes came home from his studio one night, this was two months ago, he was covered in sawdust, the sawdust clung to his skin and his clothes, it was trapped in his eyelashes. Wes bumped into everything, he tripped over everything, he dropped his keys, his bike clattered to the floor, he was not meant to be in-doors. He found me at my desk. We had moved my desk into an alcove at the rear of our apartment, where the apartment slanted toward the lake. I wondered when our building would just crack and buckle on the one side, and give itself in a cloud of dust to the water. Through the small back window, I had a view of a single tree. It was a birch tree, and it stood there against the night looking back at me across time like a piece of lightning. And Wes said, You're writing. He sank to his knees and said, You've re-entered the atmosphere. Then Wes left me alone, and he did not make a sound.

It was so quiet in the washroom of that low-level office building. Normally the halls were teeming with fragrant, neatly dressed people heading this way and that, folders clutched to their chests, but now there was no movement, no footfall. It was as if the building had been emptied, and I was the only one in the building. An apocalypse had happened, and I had missed the apocalypse. I pulled the paper towel from the dispenser, dried my face, and went into the last stall. I locked the door and hung my coat from the hook. I unwrapped the stiff plastic seal around the pregnancy test. The dimensions were too similar to a tampon's. The designer should have thought of that. Of course, men could piss in the open. Men did not bleed, they did not administer pregnancy tests, they stood there shaking their dicks at urinals, urinals which were oddly uterine-shaped, as if to say, what do you want me to do about it? I could hear the blood pound in my ears, and felt for a moment I could faint. I sat down on the closed toilet seat and put my head between my knees, made fists. Had I had enough to eat that morning? Not really.

Had I had enough water? Drinking water was boring. My hair dragged along the bleached floor. I knew someday I would read the detail I'd told Paul at the restaurant, about smelling the glue binding the slats of wood, in a novel of his, as if he had pulled that detail from the sensitive sprawl of his mind. Wes would tell me to be careful when I met with Paul, Wes would remind me that I was a writer too, to keep certain thoughts to myself. Eventually, I held the stick and peed on it. I waited in the empty washroom of the empty office building of the empty city. And then I watched as two lines sharpened in the slot, one line and then the second line as if to underscore the result. Rotate the stick and it was an equal sign. I was pregnant.

I turned on my phone. My phone came to life. It buzzed continuously, and I thought, It's Wes, it's Wes being telepathic. What Virginia Woolf wrote in her diaries, what I'd misquoted to Ani was: *I dig out beautiful caves behind my characters: I think that gives exactly what I want; humanity, humour, depth. The idea is that the caves shall connect, and each comes to daylight at the present moment.* It was not Wes. It couldn't be Wes. Wes was in New York. He was doing his big audition. I would hear from Wes later. It was Paul. There were about fifteen messages from Paul. Why was I ignoring him? After everything we had been through together. He was in the city. He needed me. It was urgent. Why was I ignoring him? What had he done?

—

I texted Paul, I would call him in a few minutes, I was sorry, my phone had been powered down, hang in there.

I put the positive pregnancy test back inside its stiff plastic wrapping, and tucked it into my coat pocket. I flushed the toilet, pulled on my army coat, zipped it to the neck, and opened the stall door.

There was a lineup of women the length of the washroom, a heavy perfume scent hung in the air, the women leaned against the wall in their synthetic clothes with their purses slung over their shoulders, their arms crossed over their chests, they were waiting, they needed to empty their bodies, they needed to reapply their faces, they needed to get back to work, the lineup of women extended out into the hallway, they were waiting for me. The other two stalls were out of order, they had signs on their doors. I had not seen the taped signs. I soaped and washed my hands. I exited the washroom without looking at anyone's eyes, but I felt their eyes on me until I'd descended the two flights of stairs, pushed the front doors of the building open, and reached the street.

Paul texted an address I did not recognize. I hailed a cab and gave the driver the address. I felt sick in the cab. I asked the driver to please open the windows, he shook his head no, he had the air conditioning on. I told the driver I was pregnant. He lowered the windows. He told me to watch the

Dalai Lama's YouTube channel. It would make me feel better. Again, my phone began to buzz. It must be Paul. I answered it, and said, I'm on my way. It was the artistic director of the theatre where I had been artist-in-residence. Listen, he was saying, he had sent a bunch of emails, but it was better to talk, it was always better to talk. Had I gotten the emails? Yes. I was sorry to be out of touch, I replied, I was out of touch with everyone, everyone except my psychiatrist, I made a desperate joke. Good news, he was saying. He wanted to program the planned sequel to *Margot* for the upcoming season. He wanted to direct *Mariel*. He wanted to stage *Mariel* in the smaller space of the theatre, the long and narrow space in the theatre's lower level, formerly a bowling alley, it sat ninety bodies, give or take the set design. The script I'd shown him was in great shape, he said, it was rehearsal ready. I said I was sorry, I couldn't do it. And I would try to explain why. I told the artistic director that Mariel Hemingway didn't interest me anymore. She had too much control. Control was her way of getting through life. She reminded me too much of my younger sister, Eva. I told the artistic director I could not see myself standing under those hot lights, getting watched and being measured, maybe I had lost my nerve. No, it was something more fundamental than that, I told the artistic director, it was not just a question of nerve.

· · ·

For years, I had a recurring dream that I'd been cast as an elderly king. In the dream, I stood in the wings, watching the stage for my cue, I stood there in the wings in my bad disguise, the long white wig fitted to my head, the long white beard glued to my jaw, in my long plum-coloured robes, my burnished crown, the elderly king waiting for my entrance, thinking, No one is going to buy this.

.   .   .

Wes's favourite line in *Hamlet* is the line spoken by Ophelia's father, Polonius.

By indirections find directions out.

.   .   .

I always read the elderly king dream to be stage fright. But sitting in the back of the cab with the windows down, speeding into an unfamiliar part of the city, I read the elderly king dream to be that I was Paul playing Paul. I was Paul performing Paul and I was afraid the audience would see through me. In that moment, I saw through Paul's performance. Paul played one Paul for me and Juliet, and another for Cherry and Eva. Paul was not barricading his studio door. He was not sleeping with his shotgun. He was never on anti-anxiety medication. Paul was in the island house with Cherry and

Eva, pouring wine, overlooking the seating plan for the wedding, growing sullen, glancing from Cherry to Eva with besieged eyes, and when they asked Paul what was wrong, Paul told Cherry and Eva how angry Juliet and I were, he was constantly having to deal with our anger, we blamed him for Natasha's suicide attempt, we could not get past it, we could not accept his life with Cherry. Eva was justified in excluding us from her wedding, Paul understood her stance, we had never accepted Eva as a full sister, our anger held us back, it prevented us from loving her in the way she deserved to be loved. Paul knew that was an ugly thing to say, but that was how he felt, and Cherry and Eva were the only ones he could be truthful with.

Cherry was not the grand manipulator. Paul was the grand manipulator. Paul was the one who pitted one side against the other, he stoked the rivalry, Cherry and Eva versus me and Juliet, with Paul as the shiny prize. The king.

. . .

Paul sat cross-legged in the dirt in front of the storage facility. He was hunched forward, his head in his hands. He looked the way he felt, like a chastised boy, swamped by the disaster of his life. How could he have made such an amateur mistake? He was an idiot. He had lost everything. He was in freefall. He had a horrible headache, his mouth was dry, his body hurt. The bad wine. He smelled of discard. Here was his daughter Mona, in the back seat of a taxi. Her penetrating look, even from here, he could feel it on him. Whenever they took a photo, her face was a scowl. She refused to smile as a child. Why had she been born with such a heavy spirit? He didn't know. Children were random. All parents made the error of expecting a familiar child, a child somewhat like themselves. Mona was born a stranger, she remained a stranger. He had tried to know her, but she was unyielding. When other women were so forthcoming with Paul, parting the curtains to their minds, making a show of their insides, Mona was a mystery to him, and this made him uncomfortable, it agitated him, with Mona, he was not sure what to do, where to look, how to be. Was she shielding herself from him? Maybe. Did she feel she needed to protect herself from him? Reluctantly, he guessed so. All the windows were down in the taxi, the driver would have protested, he would have had the AC on, it was late June in the city, but Mona would have pressed the driver to lower the windows, she would want the fresh air on her face, the drama of her hair whipping in the car. She always saw herself on a screen and never in life. She was vain, unrealistic, self-serving. No. Paul had described himself. Contrary to him, Mona wanted life, she invented life, she was in the service of life. Why was Paul so hard on her? Why was he so frustrated by her presence? He wanted to punch the air and scream. When she was physically near him, he bristled. Whenever they met for a meal, the moment she arrived, Paul laid into her. He criticized her, he took her down many notches when she was already a wet-eyed shadow of gloom. It was a game they played. He would insult her dress, her hair, her bag, her lateness. She expected his insults, and in turn, she made herself smaller, less visible to him. He was mean and biting, and because of that, she worked harder and harder, she apologized for her mess, she took his blame. He was not so different from Cherry. He toyed with love as if it were weather, he made one room bright for Juliet, the other room stormy for Mona. He shunned Mona because Mona was filled with a disease. It was the disease of her gaping love for him. He did not know what to do with it.

Paul scraped down further and further inside himself.

Why wasn't he paying her taxi fare? Why was he not moving to pay her taxi fare?

The only reason he had decent things was because Cherry was rich.

He liked all of his decent things.

A life of comfort was like a life of affection. When he dressed, he felt the affection of his clothing. When he drank, he felt the affection of his wine glass. He looked at his art and his art looked back at him. He lay on his couch, and his couch held him.

He was a kept man. He was his height and his dick and his eye colour. He was his brush with fame.

Mona was still talking to the taxi driver because she was a better and more curious person than he was.

Paul had it inside out. He was the one trying to impress Mona. He handed his secrets and confusion over to Mona like gemstones.

Mona married Wes. Wes was Paul's opposite.

Natasha described their apartment as condemned. She said she never took her coat off in their apartment.

Paul had never seen Mona's apartment. What was wrong with him that he did not want to see where his daughter lived?

Natasha married his closest friend. His only friend.

Paul watched Judd with Mona when she was a girl. Paul felt impatient with Mona and was often short-tempered with her. They clashed. Paul gave off a feeling of disappointment in her. She was not who he wanted, she was not enough, and

Paul gave excess attention to Juliet, who drank it in. It was straightforward with Juliet. Paul liked who he was with Juliet and so he went toward Juliet. It was a matter of chemistry. Mona was anti-magnetic with Paul. But whenever she saw Judd, Mona's face opened, and their companionability felt like scorn to Paul. From a distance, Paul watched Judd inhabit his life more naturally than he ever did. Over time, Paul felt as if he were the visitor, not Judd, and that there would be a point in the night when Paul would be the one to leave. When Natasha proposed they make Judd Mona's godfather, Paul feigned enthusiasm, but inside, her words cut to the bone. He felt jealous, bitter, overlooked, underloved. *Godfather*, a real step up from *father*.

Was Mona expecting Paul to pay her fare? Was she stalling in the back seat of the cab so he would come to her rescue? Paul smiled meekly in the direction of Mona's outline. He did not even know where he was going to spend the night.

Sigrid's apartment was bleak. There was no other word for it. It held the light of a permanent rainstorm. There were too many small dogs in Sigrid's suburban neighbourhood. Paul heard them barking through the walls, splitting the stale air like a power tool left on. Whenever he walked near Sigrid's, the small dogs of the neighbourhood lunged for him, and barked accusingly. The owners didn't even apologize, which Paul found ignorant and vulgar. Paul was frightened of the small dogs in Sigrid's neighbourhood. What did they see? Why did they hate only him? Sigrid kept her books on her windowsill because there was nowhere else to put them. Her books were water-stained and warped and moulding because she did not have a proper shelf. Paul could have built a proper shelf for Sigrid, he saw where the shelf could go, just above her couch, on that bare turquoise wall, but he did not want to build the shelf because Sigrid would have overvalued it, she would have seen the shelf as the break in the clouds, the evidence Paul was there to stay, and because of the shelf, she would hold Paul to a future with her. Sigrid was always congested. It was probably the dampness in the apartment. Or the bus stop in front, the bus braking there every fifteen minutes, spewing the poison of its exhaust into her rooms. She cooked, but not well. Her food was cheap. She bought it at the bulk food depot near her house, and wheeled it back to her unremarkable front door like a widow. She boiled their meat. Just once, Paul wanted to put his clothes back on after fucking Sigrid without smelling like boiled meat. From the other side of her fold-out table, he smiled at Sigrid, he told her things across the murk, he complimented her. He sat there and he tried, he looked for the code, the code to feeling. She had a beautiful body, a tangle of pale hair, she was like a Renaissance painting, she was always nude, or in an old grey cardigan sweater of his, reaching for the handkerchief in her pocket. Sigrid acquiesced too much, they never fought.

She rubbed his feet. He was gruff with her. He didn't like his face in the small square of her bathroom mirror, behind the mirror was her medicine cabinet, in it, her birth control pills, when before he had been broad-cheeked, his face was too slender now, his face carried the memory of handsomeness rather than handsomeness itself. His face was like a rose curling inward. Paul had a hollow in himself that he was trying to fill. The small dogs of the neighbourhood sensed the hollow, and with their voice boxes, they sounded the alarm. Love spilled through Paul. Sigrid's apartment was not a basement apartment, but it was not above ground either. It was the midpoint, which meant they were always in semi-darkness.

Mona used to talk to him. When he was with Lee, Mona talked to him, and Paul heard what she said as lines. He transposed her lines and he stuffed them into the mouths of the women in his books, his unpublished books, they were good lines, like neural pathways, they were the good lines of searching women. He wanted to bottle Mona like a perfume. He wanted to keep her in a room and have her talk to him. He wanted to own Mona, and the source of her good lines. One night, two winters ago, Paul cried as he listened to Mona. They were on the phone together. He was at his ski chalet. Mona was speaking in spirals. She had just lost her pregnancy, and her suffering was incomprehensible to him. He would never have an experience so transforming and sad. Paul cried as he listened to the sound of his daughter's grief, the way it held her in place, kept her dizzy, how her mind could not outsmart it, Paul cried for his daughter, but he also cried for himself. He cried for all the life he would never feel and never know, he would never know life as deeply and cruelly as his daughter had. Paul saw his reflection in his wide blackened window. Outside, snow pinpricked the night. It flew in violent gusts toward and away from Paul, and something stirred in Paul, something shifted. Paul grabbed the tape recorder off his dresser, and in the dark room, he began recording his daughter.

Now she was walking toward him on the industrial road in that surplus coat. The coat was far too big for her frame, she had always been thin as a stick. Her hair needed a trim, if only she would pull it off her face. Her complexion was sickly. There was something medieval about it. The directness in her stride, was she angry with him too? Was she going to slap him? Berate him for his shortcomings? Curse his name to hell? It was not as if Paul did not know pain. It was that, in Mona's presence, Paul's pain felt insufficient. His pain felt insufficiently known. He did not know pain the way his daughter did, and this knowledge made her superior. There she was, studying life. Paul came to stand. His joints cracked like gunfire. Everyone remarked on their resemblance, and Paul took pride when this comment was made. Paul saw what happened when Mona entered a room, the way other men looked at her. Nervously, Paul ruffled his hair. He did not know how to look at his daughter.

Sorry, Mona said flatly, kissing Paul's cheek, my driver wanted to show me a YouTube video, and her statement was like a dart in Paul's solar plexus. The Dalai Lama, Mona said. And Paul told himself to flip his mood. Because of Sigrid, he had been listening to a meditation app, and he liked this idea that every moment occurred anew.

.   .   .

Paul led me toward the mammoth building. Above us, clouds sprinted across the blue sky. Upon entering, we passed a metal door with *MANAGER* on it though the second *A* had fallen so it read *MANGER*. A woman sat in the office gazing into a small black-and-white television. When we walked by, she waved, her hand nicotine-yellow. Love will tear us apart, Paul said, winking at the manager, and from her pocket, without breaking eye contact with Paul, she retrieved an inhaler and took a short, sharp puff. It sounded like a valve twisting open. We walked the concrete corridors of the vast building. Above us, harsh fluorescent tubes of light blinked on and off. The building was cold and tunnel-like and we passed steel door after steel door until finally Paul came to a stop, and with a melancholic show of strength, hoisted open the door to his storage locker. He then stepped back into the life he had abandoned with me, Juliet and Natasha. Queasily, I followed.

Despite the lightless conditions, the cold north wind, the bottle-green sky that warned of an incoming storm, Paul was forced off the island the afternoon his secret phone was discovered. It was the Book of Revelation out there, Paul said to me, recounting his boat trip back to the mainland the day before. He came close to capsizing twice. The swells were so angry, the ocean so wild, he could hardly cut a course through it, and at one point, considered mooring the boat to a channel marker, sheltering in the bow, and taking what came for him. Paul said he had seen his death, and this was not it. His death was bloodier than drowning. Drowning was too peaceful. Drowning would not be how he met his maker. His maker had other plans, and they were gory. He had looked into the eyes of his fate, and maybe this was why he'd been so reckless with those who mattered. He didn't know. He needed to be washed clean. As Paul spoke, his words sounded increasingly familiar to me. I realized he was quoting the anti-hero of a Western I'd seen recently. Paul was borrowing the anti-hero's epiphany. Paul went on, in his own words now. Halfway to the mainland, the skies cracked open and the rain began. A hard, driving rain, it sloshed the windshield, it blinded him, he bargained with the rain. Then lightning forked the sky, the lightning was my nervous system, Paul said, I had to keep my head on, I saw that

I wanted to live, I needed to get to shore. Thunder boomed. The water tossed him viciously. I got pummelled, Paul said. I got such a scare, Paul said. Look, I'm still trembling, and Paul held his hands out, hungover, palms up. Paul was unshaven with blue hollows beneath his eyes. His clothes were stiff with dried sweat and emotion. Loose pillows were snaked along the cement ground. Paul had spent the night in the storage locker. Why hadn't he gotten a hotel room? Maybe Cherry had blocked his cards, and he was living off what was left in his money clip. Who knows how they arranged things between them. Beside the makeshift bed, there was a jug of water, a few empty bottles of wine upright like old trophies, some half-finished takeout.

You can stay at our place, I said.

No, Paul said.

We have plenty of room, I lied.

I don't want to burden you.

It wouldn't be a burden.

It would.

Wes is out of town tonight.

Good for Wes.

It wouldn't be a burden at all.

Paul changed the subject. He'd found the key to the storage locker easily enough, Paul explained, it was left out in the open, in a drawer with other keys. It was so stagnant between him and Cherry, so brittle, Paul said, they spoke so little these days that his mind filled in too much. Maybe he had misread Cherry. When he saw the key just lying there, he felt he had misread Cherry. He had made Cherry out to be sinister in order to justify his affair with Sigrid. In fact, Paul said, he was no longer sure who his enemies were, nor his allies. Paul's eyes flitted over me with vague suspicion. He felt that when it came to Cherry, there was an undertow of resentment toward her, and he was not sure she deserved it. He did not know whether the resentment was his or ours. It was probably his guilty conscience. It had been a bad divorce. He had been brutal to Natasha. Ruthless. He had left Juliet and me unprotected. He had been selfish, unthinking, obsessed with his career. Cherry was mean. He'd seen her meanness first-hand. He did not know why he'd never intervened. He'd watched her cut me down. He was weak, he guessed. He only wanted happiness. Recently, Cherry had made a comment to Paul and Paul was still thinking about the comment. Paul had been agonizing over our exclusion from Eva's wedding. He felt it symbolized the greatest failure of his life which was the failure to create a cohesive family. In response, Cherry had said, you cannot live for your children. Paul looked at me hesitantly. He felt there was some truth to Cherry's statement. Then, Paul grew restless, something constricted in him, it was dread, he had cornered himself, he anticipated my negative response, and he needed to fend it off. He was thinking about Sigrid, Paul confessed. Sigrid was calling. She left him voice mails that were like poems. She was gentle and good the way Lee had been. On some level, he loved Sigrid, but then, what was he going to do, move to an apartment in the suburbs, and at seventy, start life again?

The night my father left us for good, the night I watched him and Juliet cry in each other's arms inside our unlit garage, Paul's car was parked beside them, packed with Paul's things. It was as if Paul drove directly here, unloaded, then went on to the house he would share with Cherry, possessionless and without a past.

    I thought you shared a storage locker with Cherry, I said.

    No.

    Oh.

    Cherry has her own storage locker.

Loose on the floor by Paul's makeshift bed was a photo. A twenty-two-year-old Natasha stood before a blur of mountains in a white dress shirt, one of Paul's, knotted at her waist, tight jeans and heeled boots that went over her knees. She was standing near their rental car at a scenic lookout. She and Paul weren't married yet. They had been together for a year. Natasha loved Paul, but found herself still searching. Should she go this way or that way? She was deciding on Paul which meant she was deciding on her life. Natasha was a writer too, and she knew Paul's work would take precedence over hers, that she would end up funnelling her work into Paul's because her time and duty would go toward the family they would make together. To be a writer you needed to be alone. Or at the very least, you needed to carve out a sense of aloneness from within. Natasha knew herself. If Natasha married Paul, and had his children, her children would be all she could see. From the other side of the camera, Paul wished Natasha could just be more fun in moments like this. They were on a road trip. They were in the mountains. The mountains were beautiful. They should be making memories. Paul planned on proposing to Natasha that night. He had the ring packed inside an empty pill vial in his toiletry kit. But now he was not sure. She had that look of worry on her face. He felt the weight of her contemplations, and they burdened him. Natasha was holding vigil over something Paul could not see. He was tired of having to read into her. They'd had sex the night before, and hadn't used protection. Was that it? Had he crossed a line? He wished she would tell him where the lines were, but instead she stranded him in a limbo of guessing. She was the subject of a portrait, and he would spend an eternity painting her and getting it wrong. They'd been drunk. Natasha had hung cherries from her ears as earrings. They'd laughed and fucked and slept. Was there a more perfect trinity? Then the next morning Paul had watched Natasha step from their bed as if it were a grave. For Natasha, that dawn in the dank motel room, something new had edged itself into her mind. It was Juliet and then farther away, it was me, we were specks and we glimmered there. We had split her consciousness. She was in the mountains with Paul, but she was with us in her mind. Now, Paul had Natasha in focus. A photograph was a performance, Paul thought to himself. Everyone knew this. Why couldn't Natasha just play her part? He lusted for Natasha, he could hardly stand being this far away from her gorgeous body. He used his camera to steal her beauty, to close the distance between them. Now, he said a bit ironically without fully comprehending why, Smile!

I tucked the photo of my mother in the mountains into my army coat pocket, and felt there the positive pregnancy test. I ran my hand over the test. I felt its solidity. I could not wait to tell Wes. I missed Wes. I wanted to get home. Wes's audition would be ending soon. I wanted to talk to Wes, I wanted the narcotic effect of his voice on me. Standing there with my father in the storage locker, I was the one exiting the frame.

Hold on, Paul said. What's your rush? He was moving to the rear of the storage locker, raising dust. He pried open a moving box and, like a bad magician, limply pulled from it the three manuscripts. They were handwritten and paper-clipped, the rubber band that held them long since snapped. Paul handed the manuscripts to me.

Give these to Judd.

Okay.

He can use them as kindling for all I care.

195

Ha.

I'm serious.

Okay.

He can roll them into logs and set them on fire.

I'll let him know.

In that awful cabin of his.

Okay.

That cheap cabin.

Okay.

That shitbox of a cabin.

It's not the cabin's fault you're here.

Thank you, Mona. Tell Judd he can do what he wants with them.

I will.

Jesus. You look ashen, Mona.

Well, I'm . . . And out of some dumb, automatic instinct, I nearly told Paul, I nearly told Paul I was pregnant before telling Wes. Why? To let him know I was miraculous? Instead, in the dark mouth of the storage locker, I said to my father, Well, I'm a writer.

Then, Paul pulled out a small black cassette player. He shook it. Batteries clunked against the sides of the plastic box. Paul pressed play. The whir of a tape. The Pretenders. *Cause I gonna make you see / There's nobody else here, no one like me—* Natasha's favourite song—*I'm special / So special.* Paul danced. I danced. Paul danced in his way with his lips pouted, his eyes closed. The music was borderless like colour, it took us elsewhere, it led us back to each other, it was always easy when we were dancing. Paul paused the song. He gazed down at the stack of manuscripts in my hands. His pupils flashed. His body became light like a child's. In the cramped cell, he looked around for a shopping bag, found one, lovingly slipped the pages inside, pulled my wrist through the handles of the bag, and said, On second thought, give these to your mother.

. . .

Why aren't we FaceTiming right now? I asked Wes, who was in New York for the night. He was back in his hotel room after his big audition. There was a pause, he put me on speaker phone, then a text came through. It was a photo of Wes, taken by Wes, standing naked in front of the hotel bathroom mirror. His right eye was blackened and swollen shut, his bottom lip gashed open. He had a bag of melting ice in his left hand, and in his right, the hand that held his phone, I could see his knuckles were slashed and raw. He had bruises and scrapes sporadically over his torso. The tendons of his neck were flexed. On the marble counter and in the basin of the bronze sink were piled the white towels and washcloths he had used to sop up his blood.

——

Three hours earlier, Wes was sitting in the holding area of the production offices in Soho. He drank a glass of cold water. This would be his fourth and final audition for the film. He was doing a screen test with the female lead. He didn't know who she was, he didn't know who the director was. The director would be in the room. The producers would be sitting in, and casting, though Wes had already met the two casting directors, and he liked them. Wes was playing the role of a junkie, a pretty junkie who hooks and steals to feed his habit. When he falls through a skylight in an attempted robbery, Wes's character is arrested by a female cop. She recruits him. To avoid jail time, he agrees to go undercover. Wes's character ends up infiltrating then breaking up a drug ring. Despite their compound damage, Wes's character and the female cop fall in love. She saves Wes's character's life. Toward the end of the film, as she is moving into the apartment she will share with Wes's character, the female cop is killed. A single bullet to the back of the head. Despite himself, Wes's character returns to the streets of New York, and in the final frame of the film, he overdoses. Wes knew the role was between him and another actor. The rumour was Gael García Bernal, but he might be too old and too short, though that might also be what made him right. Wes might be too young and too tall, though that might also be what made him right. They wanted an actor who had been recently low-profile. They wanted an actor who was a relative unknown. They wanted him to feel as if he'd come out of nowhere, as if you'd both never, but always known him. The screen test that afternoon in New York would be a chemistry test with the female lead, and it would give the director the information he needed. Wes's agent could not tell him much more than that. The project was like a secret knighthood, Wes's agent said, and it was Wes's chance at a Supporting Actor Oscar.

Wes was led into the darkened room. The lights and cameras were set up. Wes shook the hands of the casting directors, he met the producers, there were three of them, he knew their names, their faces were a blur, Wes stopped himself and memorized their faces, attached their faces to their names. Wes wore a white T-shirt and black jeans. Wes was aware of his sinewy forearms when he extended his hand to shake the producers', that his hands were large like palm leaves. On the table between them, there were cups of coffee, iPads, notepads, pens, a few bottles of water. The producers looked up at Wes and then down at their phones, and then they powered off their phones. They studied Wes. They asked Wes if he needed anything. No, no, thank you, I'm good, Wes said. In the room, they waited for the female lead and the director. The group asked Wes about his time in New York so far. He'd flown in last night? Yeah, he'd flown in last night. How was the hotel? Good, beautiful, Wes said, thank you. Had he eaten? Yes, Wes said. He'd gone to a diner near the hotel. Bacon and eggs. How did he get to the audition? Had he Ubered? If he'd Ubered he could give his receipt to reception. Production would pay for it. No, no, Wes said. I walked. Oh, cheap date, the group joked, and they laughed. They told Wes to give his breakfast receipt to reception. No, I should be paying you, Wes said. On the way here, Wes said, I saw Kathleen Turner. The group smiled and thought about *Body Heat*. She was just standing there at a stoplight like a person would stand at a stoplight. Then, Wes said, a guy waved me over and asked me if I wanted to see the moon. The guy had a telescope set up and the telescope was huge, it was the size of a rocket. The moon was so beautiful blown up. It was far more ragged and complex than the naked eye could see. I bet, one of the producers said, I bet it was. And Wes said he felt New York switched day for night, that the moon and Kathleen Turner belonged to the night. Then one of the producers asked, Is it true you play the cello? We hear you play the cello.

Wes heard a commotion on the other side of the door. Then the door opened and Rihanna walked in. Wes heard himself say, Mother of God. There was no way to describe her beauty. Wes and Rihanna shook hands, and Rihanna laughed graciously at how undone Wes was. They talked, but Wes could not remember what was said between them. It's a complete blank, Wes said. Rihanna was playing the part of the female cop. A few more minutes passed. Wes got the chance to acclimate to the room. He went over to the camera and the lighting guys, he introduced himself and they talked. One of the lighting guys wore a Rangers hat, so Wes told the camera and the lighting guys that quote about hockey being a combination of ballet and murder. They laughed at that. One of the producers was watching Wes. She liked the way he moved. He moved like geometry, she couldn't explain it. The strongest art composition was a triangle, Mona Lisa was head and elbows, Mona Lisa was a triangle. The guy made perfect shapes with his body. The guy was Mona Lisa. She told this to the producer sitting next to her, and he agreed. Yeah, the guy was a beautiful mover. They continued watching Wes. Then the door to the room was pushed open again, and everyone at the long table stood up. Wes glanced back over to Rihanna, and Rihanna was still as a statue. Rihanna and Wes watched as the thickset figure entered the room. Wes saw the motorcycle jacket first, then the black helmet gripped at the waist like a severed head. Then Wes saw the blond hair, the unruly beard. Then the director spoke. It was Magnus Beck.

.　　.　　.

God watched the fight and God loved the fight. The fight went viral. The fight was all the internet could see. A woman, an onlooker with her friend beside her, filmed it. They happened to be walking by the building when they noticed, beneath an exit light, a built guy pulling on a black motorcycle helmet and a tall, skinny guy in a tense stand-off.

.   .   .

The filmmaker crosses the street to get a closer look. The men are chest to chest, and their faces are nearly touching. They are sputtering words at each other, but it's too quiet, too guttural, we can't hear what they are saying. The filmmaker pans. We're on a sidewalk in Soho, the cobbled streets of Soho, we see the Gucci store, Celine. It is June, it is evening, the sky is purple. The filmmaker returns her focus to the men, whose faces are touching now, the tall, skinny guy's face pushes against the black visor of the built guy's motorcycle helmet. Then, without warning, the built guy winds back and punches the tall, skinny guy right in the face.

Whoa.

Dude.

The tall, skinny guy staggers backward, he nearly falls, he holds out his hands for balance, and then he puts his face in them. More onlookers gather around the men on the sidewalk. Now it is a small crowd. About ten people. Eventually, the skinny guy rights himself, he must be six foot three, and he starts to laugh. His teeth are smeared with blood. That's when more of the crowd starts filming. Almost everyone in the crowd is filming now. The original filmmaker shoots the crowd, and what we see through her lens are the diamond-white circles of the onlookers' flashes as their phones are aimed at the two men. It is a mirror ball and it is hypnotic. The filmmaker directs her camera back to the skinny guy.

He is still doubled over, still laughing, blood drips from his mouth onto the sidewalk. He touches his bleeding mouth. The helmet guy stands there like an android. The skinny guy catches his breath, he rights himself, and then he says, I can't believe you just punched me in the face with a helmet on. And the crowd makes a sound of affirmation. One of the onlookers says, Yeah, take your helmet off. And another says, Take your helmet off like a man. The Terminator takes his helmet off and he places it like a holy thing on the curved back of a nearby BMW motorcycle. That's when the skinny guy loses his shit. He runs at the built guy. The men beat on each other. Both men stumble into the cobbled street then back onto the sidewalk. They grab each other's shirts. They are kicking and throwing punches. Pushing each other up against the brick wall of the building, scraping each other's backs against the brick wall. The skinny guy is in a T-shirt, the built guy in a motorcycle jacket, the built guy's forearm is up against the skinny guy's neck, the skinny guy gets out from under the hold. He might have bitten the built guy's arm or maybe his cheek. The built guy is holding his cheek. He has one hand over his cheek. The men break apart, they are huffing. That's when the skinny guy, his eye swelling shut, the left side of his face coated in blood, says, I hear you can't sleep at night. You can't sleep at night because you're a rapist. And the crowd makes a sound of disgust. One of the onlookers says, Get him. And the skinny guy loses his shit again. The built guy mostly fends off the skinny guy.

They are punching the air now, holding their arms out, leaning against the brick wall, they are both done at this point. Then the built guy weaves his way back toward the black motorcycle. The crowd stays with the skinny guy, but the filmmaker and her friend follow the built guy. She shoots him as he gets on his motorcycle. The built guy is astride his motorcycle now and he is getting oriented, he holds his helmet, checks that he has his phone, he is a bit stunned. The filmmaker goes for a close-up, and that's when the built guy looks dead in her camera like a mug shot. Then, he pulls his helmet down over his face, fumbles with his key for a second, and drives off.

Whoa.

Jesus.

Okay.

That was that guy.

That was totally that guy.

The guy who.

He broke up what's-her-name's marriage.

Oh yes he did.

The fight.

The pool.

The white bikini.

Director guy.

Yeah. Director guy.

The one who did.

That movie.

So violent.

The movie with.

Best Picture.

Yeah.

Fucking.

Yeah.

What's his fuck.

Magnus.

Magnus Beck.

Magnus Fucking Beck.

Yeah Magnus Beck.

It's payday, Magnus Beck.

It's payday, rapist.

Magnus Beck is a rapist.

So. Wait. Sh. Hold up, hold up. Is that Adam Driver then?
Bleeding dude on the step?

No. Better looking.

Right.

Yeah.

Same feeling though.

Same feeling as Adam Driver.

Same big feeling.

Dude looks hurt.

Hot though.

Definitely.

Yeah.

In an indirect way, but hot.

I'd take a run at him.

Same.

Hey. You need help?

No. Thank you, I'm good. I'm all good.

You sure?

I'm sure.

You're beaten up pretty bad.

Yeah.

You want us to get you a car?

No. Thank you, though. That's nice.

You sure?

I'm sure. Thank you, though.

Yeah?

Yeah.

Sure?

I'm sure.

Good?

I'm good. I saw Kathleen Turner today so I'm good. And the moon. Up close. And Rihanna. Up close.

You need medical attention?

No. Ha. I'm good.

You sure?

I'm sure.

Positive?

Yeah. I can sew.

You're funny.

Thank you. I'll call my wife. She'll know what to do. But thank you. You're so nice.

What's your name?

Wes. What's yours?

.   .   .

That was the bridge.

.   .   .

Ani and I watched the fight together on her couch. We were in her coach house. We watched it with our eyes mostly shut, making Venetian blinds with our fingers. Then we watched it on mute. Then we watched it with sound. Then we watched it several times. After the fight, we closed Ani's laptop, put the warm laptop on the floor, and we lay there together on her couch. We looked like the portrait Ani painted of us at theatre school. Ani was staring up at the ceiling, I had my head turned toward Ani.

Lying on her couch together, Ani remembered our last production at theatre school. It was the production of *Hamlet* she designed. She told me that the morning after Wes broke up with her, the morning after I yelled at the director, Sonny, for the cheap, stupid way he wanted me to die, Ani woke up. I was asleep beside her in her bed. She remembered the night before and Wes's painful words and she was flooded with fresh humiliation, but the humiliation acted on her like a pressure, and Ani got out of bed. She dressed quickly and walked down to the theatre. She remembered the light her father's soul gave off as it hovered above her, changing shape in his bedroom. He was on his bed and she was close by on a stuffed armchair unsure of what to do other than watch him. I didn't even hold his hand, Ani said. Her father's cigar had gone out, it had fallen from his mouth and burned a small black hole in his shirt. He had the newspaper in his lap, his reading glasses on, his feet were crossed at the ankle. Her mother was out at a restaurant. Ani did not think to call her mother. Ani had come into the room to watch television. Her father's eyes were open, but his chest didn't move. You could say he was gazing into eternity, but you would be wrong. He was not gazing into anything. He was dead. There was no dimension to him. Life had exited his body. Then the light was there. It was directly above her father, Ani said, and it was very beautiful. The light in the room was iridescent, the closest thing to it on earth would be a giant soap bubble, Ani said, it was liquid. It was the colour of memory, the memory of a life. We think of light as fleeting, but this was the opposite. It had form and it had matter, Ani said, it was my father telling me to remember beauty and to be changed by it. It was our dark day so Ani had the theatre to herself. She said she played around with lighting effects. She used a blowtorch, a magnifying glass and cellophane wrap.

I tried not to burn the theatre down, Ani said. For my death scene as Ophelia, she tried to recreate what she had seen in the room where her father died. It was impossible, Ani said. But it felt so good to try. To be back there with him again.

Ani's mother, Marilyn, was in the next room reading *Vogue*. Marilyn did not want to see Wes's fight. She hated violence. She lived with Ani now in Ani's coach house. Ani said they'd gone to the dog park earlier that day, and their dog, a husky mix, had been exuberant, and a stranger judged their dog and said to Ani, Why can't you just get it together? Ani looked down. Her stockings were ripped. Marilyn had her keys around her neck, a hospital bracelet, her shirt unbuttoned. Ani asked the stranger, Why are you so angry? And Ani began to shake when she told me this. She said she felt infected by the stranger's anger. It was when she and Marilyn were leaving the dog park with their dog, Miss World, that Ani saw the stranger was Cherry. In all our years of friendship, Ani had met Cherry only once. During what we called a peace time, just before Ani and I went to theatre school, Ani had come with me to Paul and Cherry's big house for dinner.

What Ani had never told Mona about that night was that when Ani left the dinner table and walked the cavernous hallways to the restroom, taking in the art on the walls, noting the seated portraits of Cherry's sons, of Eva, there was no physical evidence of Mona or Juliet in that big house, Paul followed Ani. He was drunk, just in balance. Paul grinned at Ani then floated his face to hers. Standing close to Paul was like standing close to Jupiter. Ani felt a rush. She was tempted. Like everyone, she had read *Daughter*. Paul told Ani that he saw her hunger. He saw the way she wanted to get nearer to the workings of the universe. He saw her cool intensity. She was a conclusive person. She lived without regret, Paul said, and he admired that. Ani and Paul half-swayed in the hallway. Ani wondered if Paul wasn't reciting a passage from *Daughter*. Ani was an introvert. She did not understand the sport of sociability. At the dinner table, Ani felt like her ribs were being pried open. Question after question, it was relentless. Ani had gone to the restroom because she needed a break. She needed to feel the contours of herself, the hushed reservoir of her mind. Talking had never done her any good. When Ani returned to the dinner table, Paul kept his eyes from hers for the remainder of the night. She had rejected his advances. She felt his love was staged, even for Mona. When Cherry and Paul left the table to get something, more wine or maybe it was dessert, Ani watched Mona slip some of their silver into her bag. Then Mona took the salt shaker. Once they started laughing it was impossible to stop. Mona reached for Ani's hand, and that was when Mona's hair caught fire on the tall candles burning in the centre of the table. Ani clapped Mona's hair until the flames went out.

—

In the coach house, Miss World came to lie on Ani's strong body, her paw around Ani's wrist like a bangle. I told Ani that Paul had mentioned Cherry had recently bought a dog. The dog was a purebred, and like their couch, flown in from France. Ani and I agreed that when you don't have a mother—not because she is dead, but because you actively cut yourself off from her—when you don't have a mother, you can never fully rest. Ani and I agreed that motherhood was vigilance. Without a mother, you had to take that role on for yourself. For a second, we thought about Cherry, and we felt sorry for her.

Ani's phone buzzed. Some dick to break up the day, Ani said and she showed me the dick that filled her screen, the dick with its slight curve to the left. Ani raised her eyebrows in appraisal. That's how men talk now, Ani said. Dick pics. Language is dead.

Siri short for serial killer.

Yeah.

When I was leaving, I went into the other room. Marilyn was wearing the pearl necklace I had given her, it was the pearl necklace I had stolen from Cherry. Marilyn took my hands in hers and said, Look out for each other, not just for now, but for life.

. . .

I was standing in the airport by Wes's gate. I was a few minutes early, eating saltines from the box. My phone buzzed. It was Ani. She texted an old photo of Dolly Parton. Such sunshine, Ani wrote beneath the photo. Around me, people held balloons and flowers. The gates opened and Wes was there. I winced when I saw his injured face. He wore an *I Love New York* T-shirt. His other shirt would have been wrecked in the fight. His wrinkled black jeans, his half-empty gym bag, he never packed anything, he didn't think about rain or shampoo. I put the saltine box in my army coat pocket and lifted my sign, *WES IS MORE*. Wes came loping toward me. In the centre of that bright, frantic space, we held on to each other. I spoke the fact into his ear, I'm pregnant.

It hurts to smile, Wes said.

.   .   .

Wes's agent sent Wes a bouquet after the fight went viral, congratulating Wes on his Best Supporting Actor win.

.   .   .

Magnus went into hiding.

Twenty-two women came forward.

—

Every studio head made a statement disavowing their relationship to Magnus Beck. Magnus Beck was dropped from all projects, both future and current.

David Lynch stood with the women who came forward.

His hair was even better IRL.

So did the lead actress who had been photographed fighting with Magnus by the pool.

Magnus's wife filed for divorce. She got sole custody of their dog, Anaïs Nin.

On a minor highway in upstate New York, on a clear stretch of road on a clear day, Magnus Beck lost control of his motorcycle and crashed into a utility truck. Debris was spread over half a mile of highway. Magnus Beck walked away from the crash, and went back into hiding until his court date.

. . .

When Cherry pushed open the front door, she called out Paul's name. She'd forbidden him from staying at the house, but thought she would find him there anyway. He was soft. Where else would he go? Cherry did not want to answer that. She entered the security code into the panel, and the system chimed for Cherry. It was deactivated. *Paul*. She called Paul's name again, and heard the strain of her own voice in the foyer. Her voice was thin. She was alone. Paul was not there. The house was empty. It smelled faintly of rot. The odour intensified as Cherry got closer to the kitchen. Cherry knotted the garbage bag, took it out of the house, dropped it into the bin, and secured the lid. She dragged the metal bin to the curb. There were her next-door neighbours getting into their ugly car with their strange, nervous child. Cherry ignored them. They were the ones who had erected the backyard fence so high Cherry felt imprisoned by it. For weeks, after it was built, after their disagreement, Cherry walked the perimeter of her yard in circles, like an inmate, always in the same bitter, clockwise direction. There was no other way she could make her point about the fence, the fence, she understood from the inspector who'd been sent by the city, and later, his supervisor, was up to code. The problem with the fence was that it reduced Cherry's direct sun. Flowers needed sun. Cherry needed sun. Paul was probably in his girlfriend's basement apartment, having sex in her shower, and this thought caused Cherry physical pain.

Cherry had come into the city. A few days after the discovery of the secret phone, she decided she needed to come in. This was why Ani had seen Cherry in the dog park. Would Cherry confront Paul? She didn't know. Would they reconcile? Maybe. She was not sure she could go through it again, the act of forgiving Paul. Forgiveness was a very physical act, Cherry felt, it was an exertion like a labour or an amputation. People made the mistake of reducing forgiveness to an intellectual exercise. A thing you told your mind to do. It was not. She could attest to that with certainty. Cherry replayed the stream of messages between Paul and his young, literary girlfriend. They were pornography. The young woman had sent Paul photos of her body parts, where she curved inward and outward. She was young and pretty with long greasy hair. She probably made her own wooden shoes and had a clear, plastic shower curtain. She probably kept her books on a windowsill and let them curl and spot with mildew. She had nothing to care for but Paul. Cherry tried to scrub the pictures from her mind, and the effort was so overwhelming, it quickly filled Cherry with an inconsolable ache. Cherry sat down on the couch beneath the darkened square left by the Rothko. She let her eyes close. Something was missing. So much was missing. She had forgotten the dog. The dog was in the back of the car. Cherry ran out into the driveway and unlocked the trunk of the station wagon. There was Antoine, coming to life upon seeing Cherry, dead without her. People looked at Cherry as if she were a hateful woman. If only they could hear her now. The cooing, doting voice she used with Antoine, it was a language Cherry spoke only to him. She led the dog to the prison yard, and re-entered the house.

—

The icemaker in the new fridge delivered the ice cubes in such an elegant shape.

She dropped three ice cubes into her glass and poured some mineral water over them.

She sipped.

She leaned against the stainless-steel counter.

Cherry had never really had friends. She did not see the point. She thought friendship was middle ground, like a spritzer. When things went wrong, Cherry had only herself to rely on. There was no one to call, no one to sit with her, and tell her she was right, Paul was wrong, she did not deserve to be treated like a pest in the dirt, like a pigeon, like a squirrel, like some filthy everyday thing. There was a period when Cherry grew close to her hairdresser. Her hairdresser confided in Cherry that her husband was a chronic cheat, a bad boy, but she kept taking him back. Love was blind. Soon, Cherry came in for weekly appointments. Her hairdresser had talked Cherry into a layered cut, which in retrospect, Cherry felt was too high-maintenance for her textured hair and a cheap ploy to make Cherry a regular. The hairdresser's hard touch on her scalp felt so good. When Cherry thought of her touch now, she thought of the expression *the laying on of hands*. She dug into Cherry's head with her fingertips, then warmed her with the desert wind of the blow dryer. Cherry let her eyes close. She listened to her hairdresser's problems which were also her problems. How would she solve them, what would she do? After a few months of weekly contact, the hairdresser told Cherry she had finally left her low-life husband. Cherry felt shocked, saddened, betrayed. She hid her emotions, and lauded her hairdresser. She told her how brave she was for striking out on her own. But, her hairdresser added somewhat mournfully, she was now struggling to save up for a down payment on a house. In that moment Cherry saw the friendship for what it was. The hairdresser was a con, she was after Cherry's money, nothing more. Cherry lashed out. She insulted the hairdresser, her studded jeans, her made-up face, the piece of fried chicken in her purse, she exuded desperation, she was a pathetic woman. Cherry had an outburst in the salon. She left in the salon's black robe with wet hair. Later, the salon called Cherry to say there had been a misunderstanding. The hairdresser had only the best of intentions. She had worked at the salon since it opened. She was undeserving of Cherry's attack. It had been unfair of Cherry to speak to her the way that she did. Cherry's business was no longer welcome there.

Cherry's phone buzzed.

Cherry gave herself a moment before looking at it.

—

It would be Paul.

They had a line between them. However far they managed to drift apart, Cherry found she was still holding her end of the line.

She had not heard from Paul since his dramatic departure from the island. She had tried to reason with him, she followed him into the boathouse, pleaded he not go, the conditions were far too dangerous, he would get thrown, *my father, please*. But after a struggle, Paul set Cherry aside. He carried on as if she were not there. Mechanically, he went from ring to ring, unfastening the ropes, releasing the boat from its moorings. Forty minutes later, Cherry called the marina, her heart was in her throat, she could hardly get her question out. The marina confirmed Paul had arrived in one piece. He'd just driven off for the city.

When Cherry updated Eva, Eva had said she wished Paul was dead. It would be so much easier to be fatherless.

Cherry saw now that Paul had made a show of his departure from the island to recover his power over Cherry. Paul weakened Cherry by reminding her of her love for him.

He made her, unmade her.

—

The first time she saw Paul, she loved him instantly. He was reading from a work in progress for a fundraiser, a black-tie. Cherry's husband was with her, but he was like a cardboard box beside her. She had no feeling for him. She advanced through the crowd to introduce herself to Paul. It was not as if she lived outside the bounds of romance.

Cherry looked over at the promising black rectangle of her phone.

Her phone looked back at her. Her phone was her friend.

Paul will go one of two ways, Cherry. Either he will be cold and withholding, making you the one to work to get him back. This is not acceptable, Cherry. Or, he will grovel and seduce and pledge purity of heart, say he is sorry and he is returned. This is what you deserve, Cherry.

Cherry played out this version of Paul, repentant Paul. She did not have the stamina for the other version of Paul, mean Paul, the Paul who behaved as if nothing had ever happened between them, they had never fallen in love, they had never had a daughter, they had never made a life.

Cherry looked at her phone. The text was from the florist for Eva's wedding. The florist and her appeals. She was insisting the floral arrangements and the crown be driven north in a refrigerated truck. Cherry knew the refrigerated truck was an attempt to gouge her. The florist argued that the flowers needed to be refrigerated for the long drive or they risked dying. Cherry looked out at her garden. It was a sweltering day. Her garden was alive. She texted the florist to say she would Uber the flowers.

Cherry checked the value of her art. She checked the real estate value of her properties. The city house, the ski chalet, the island home. All of it, rising. Even the Rothko.

Cherry Googled her hairdresser.

She had remarried. The new husband was a father of two. Daughters. And her hairdresser loved them like her own. Heart emoji. Heart emoji.

That first trip to Spain with Paul's girls, Cherry had turned a garden hose on Mona. Paul was at the kitchen window, watching himself watch the incident.

The sun burned. The sea was green. The children were in the large yard of the rental house spread out like mental patients. Cherry's sons played rigidly beneath a tree. Juliet lay sun-oiled in the grass while Mona, stomach-down in a depressing bikini, made notes in the margins of a library book. The Mediterranean glinted at their backs. Cherry was

pregnant with Paul's child. She knew the child was excep-
tional, the child would keep her and Paul together. It had
not been easy. Paul romanticized the past, he wrestled with
his guilt. Cherry told Paul, If that life was so preferable to
this one, you should just go back to it. It's not like I'm bar-
ring the exits. Natasha was so prevalent in Paul's mind,
Paul had recently called Cherry *Tash*. He never said Cherry's
name this way, soaked in devotion and awe. He said Cherry's
name as if he were still learning how to pronounce it, as if
her name were a thing to hitch to the end of a plea. A garden
hose was coiled at Cherry's feet. She picked it up with no
particular forethought. She simply needed something heavy
in her hands, an object to absorb and dissipate her energy.
When Mona began to cross the yard toward the house, Cherry
switched on the water. She felt its ice-cold jet against her
fingertip, and as Mona passed Cherry without so much as a
glance, she drove the jet into Mona's torso, her face and then
her back. Cherry did not break into a run, but she did chase
Mona with the garden hose. *Just drown*. Cherry said this.

Cherry recalled the aftermath. Mona and Juliet dripping
water through the rental house, their bare feet skidding
over the tile floors, making them impassable. Paul, in un-
steady pursuit, asking *what happened* when he very well knew
the answer. His daughters stuffing their travel bags with
their department store clothes while Paul said empty things
that sounded full. Juliet raged. Mona did not. Mona kept her

face sphinxlike. Mona was always watching, never joining. She made an art out of her exclusion. Once the girls were packed, they stood in the arched doorway with Paul. Cherry approached the doorway. Mona told Cherry *Go fuck yourself until the end of time.* Paul chided Mona. He apologized to Cherry. It was a shock to hear Mona swear. Juliet was the one with the foul mouth. Cherry watched Paul's girls leave the rental house, their bags packed so hastily they looked like misshapen growths on their backs. The girls rearranged their growths, shifting them from one shoulder to the other, and walked in the direction of Cherry's brother's. If her brother took them in, Cherry would never speak to him again. Loyalty was an ongoing trial. Not just of the other person, but of yourself. To estrange yourself from a disloyal sibling was a sign of self-respect. Self-respect and self-preservation were one and the same. She transmuted these thoughts to her unborn child, praying for a girl who would outdo all girls.

Paul's daughters left. He stayed.

Call me *Cher*, Cherry suggested to Paul that night. *Cher*, Paul echoed. Cherry was right. With Paul, Cherry was always right. It was her rightness that kept her alive. Her rightness was the flame in her chest.

A bang on the glass. It was Antoine. Cherry let him into the house. She wiped his paws with an old towel. She understood why Barbra Streisand had her dog cloned. Antoine busied himself at Cherry's feet then came to lie on the floor and pant. Cherry refilled his water bowl. He must be hot under that coat. She went up to her bedroom. She listened to the smack of her low heels as she climbed the stairs in the hollow shell of her house.

Cherry lay on her bed. If her body suddenly stopped working the way her mother's had, if one of her organs exploded abruptly, her heart, how long would it be before her body was discovered?

Who would discover her body?

Her next-door neighbours?

What did a woman have to do to get noticed?

Just before her first son was born, Cherry told her mother she was frightened of the pain of childbirth. In response, Cherry's mother said, The only way to get over pain is to tolerate it.

It was months after the baby was born that Cherry's mother first came to visit. Cherry looked back on those early, sleepless months and felt she spent them in a state of suspension, not with her new baby, but waiting for her mother.

The day of her mother's visit, Cherry stood at her front window and peered out. It was humid, the air was heavy. There was not enough air. At the appointed time, Cherry watched her mother's driver slow to a stop in front of her house. Her mother got out of the car, bent forward like an omen. Near Cherry, in his bassinet, the baby fussed. Cherry did not know how to hold him, she did not know what words to use to soothe him. The baby was a stranger living in her house. She toiled day and night. The closer a woman got to a newborn, the more worthless she became. Her mother told Cherry she would not be staying long. She handed Cherry a blanket, saying it was her gift to the baby. Cherry recognized the blanket from her mother's country house. It was stained and had been pitted by bugs, it would surely smother the baby. The baby cried. Cherry looked into the open black mouth of this boy. She tried to rock him, but he flexed and squirmed, she tried to shush him. Cherry felt like a moth bashing herself against the light. She looked over at her mother apologetically. Her mother watched her from a distance. She sat there and Cherry saw only judgment in her mother's eyes. Her mother covered her ears. She could not stand the baby's mewling cries. She asked Cherry for a glass of wine. The wine relaxed her mother so Cherry poured it for her, and refilled her glass, the baby cried himself unconscious. Cherry's mother spoke only about Cherry's brother. He was making something of himself.

—

Cherry went over to Paul's dresser. She started going through his top right-hand drawer, the drawer where he kept his personal things, sentimental things, a champagne cork from the night *Daughter* was launched, along with the scraps of his life, loose change, ballpoint pens, money clips. In the mess, Cherry could see a photo, black and white, tucked carefully inside a piece of tracing paper. A woman. Cherry pulled the photo from the tracing paper. Mona. She looked directly, wearily into the camera. Something heavy in her eyelids. A hangover, a love affair, a secret. Who knows. Everyone made such a big deal out of Mona when she was obviously so common. In the photo, her hair was dark and unbrushed. She wore a coat and beneath it, a sweater. The photo must have been taken when Mona was at theatre school. Mona would have blotted this from her mind, but it was Cherry who'd been the first to tell Mona she should act, she should write, it was Cherry who'd first told Mona, You have a gift.

Mona.

Looking at her face had always been unbearable.

It eroded Cherry.

I am someone's daughter too, Cherry thought to herself.

—

Cherry went back to the opening night of *Margot*. That day, she had followed Paul around the house, she had pestered Paul to be sure Mona had reserved a seat for her next to him, had he texted Mona, had he called her, had he texted, text again, call, was he sure.

When it was time to go to the theatre, Cherry sat in their living room with the lights off. She said she had a headache. And she pictured Mona making her entrance, looking out from the stage at the vacant seat next to Paul, staring back blank and penetrating as hatred, in the middle of the front row.

Cherry slammed the dresser drawer shut.

Antoine barked.

He was barking.

Cherry heard his claws skittering up the stairs.

Could he hurt himself? Could a dog lose his balance and fall down the stairs? Cherry flung her body toward the doorway, and then to the top of the stairwell, but it was not Antoine, it was Paul who was there, Paul who was climbing the stairs in his loafers to see Cherry, to see if she was alright. Hadn't she heard him? He'd been calling her name.

. . .

For the time being, Paul wrote to me and Juliet, he was sleeping in the storage locker. We were not to worry about him. He was fine. He had come to an arrangement with the manager. Turned out she was a fan. Paul confided he had seen both Cherry and Sigrid over the last two days, and felt no closer to a resolution. Eva's wedding was in a few weeks. Eva was calling and texting. Her bombardment was creating a lot of stress for Paul. Weddings were like diagrams, Eva was telling Paul. His absence would make her wedding asymmetrical. She wanted a *symmetrical* wedding. She needed to know if Paul was attending. If he was not attending, she would tap another man to walk her down the aisle. Paul was replaceable. Eva did not have to feel love for Paul, but she did have to convey the appearance of love on her wedding day. Her guests were expecting love and she wanted to exceed their expectations. Would he be there or not? At the same time, Cherry argued that if Paul left her, he might improve his relationship with me and Juliet, but he would lose his relationship with Cherry and Eva.

Either way, Juliet wrote to Paul, you will lose something. If you leave Cherry, you will lose us. Not that we would ever withhold ourselves from you, but because the structure of your family is built on our exclusion. Juliet wrote that she felt real pain at the prospect of Paul returning to Cherry and all that symbolized. She thought he had hit his point of no return. The outcome seemed inevitable given that he was living this double life again. Was it not? If Paul forfeited the good love, Sigrid, out of some morbid fear of Cherry, did that not expose the true underpinnings of his relationship to Cherry? Do you not see that you are repeating a cycle? Juliet wrote to Paul. You were in the same bind three years ago with Lee. You dragged us through it then. You are dragging us through it now. Look through our lens for once.

I did not tell Paul about my pregnancy. I did not tell Natasha because I didn't want my mother to agonize over my state. I told Juliet. Juliet knew everything. My pregnancy was my world beneath the world. In my mind, my lost child lived beside my growing child. I rejected the idea that grief was a thing to *get over*. That it was a failure of your will if you did not *get over* your grief. Natasha was right. Grief was generative. I went between our bed and my desk. I wrote until my fingertips went numb.

I swore to myself this time I would be clear-eyed with Paul. I texted Juliet to say it was all feeling familiar in the wrong way. If Paul went back to Cherry, we had to liberate ourselves from the pattern. You need to swear to me, I texted Juliet.

I swear, Juliet texted back.

—

But my heart weakened when Paul got in touch. Paul called, I picked up. He emailed, I responded. *I want to see you in a regular way, Mona, the way a father sees his daughter. I am tired of meeting in restaurants.* I wanted peace with my father. I wanted him to atone for the hurts of the past. He had come so close with Lee. He was even closer now with Sigrid. *How can I have a relationship with Sigrid if I love Cherry? If I love Cherry, shouldn't a relationship with Sigrid be impossible? I must not love Cherry.* I told myself to be careful, you know how Paul is. Do not open yourself the way you did the last time. Paul is the atmospheric disturbance, the high wind slamming you to the ground. Paul is in it only for himself.

But is he?

He is my *father.*

Paul wrote to me and Juliet. He had gone to Sigrid's for a few days. He was sick. Some kind of bronchial infection. He did not know whether the love with Sigrid was real. He had gone to her place to put their love to the test. What would it be like to live with Sigrid in an ordinary way, to read different books in the same room, to lie beside her at night and cough? Paul wrote that Sigrid kept looking over at him. She could concentrate on nothing but Paul. When Paul was near, the world dropped away. Sigrid shone with happiness. It unnerved him. She got nosebleeds. Sigrid would be at the stove, stirring some coarse mixture in a huge pot, turn around, and blood would be spilling from her nose to her lips. At the sight of Paul, she would smile through the blood. She was always in the nude. Her spine was like a rosary. I don't know, Paul wrote. Is this *a life*? After three days, Paul wrote, he felt the love with Sigrid was more fantastical than real, and was it not selfish of Paul to subject Sigrid to a fantastical love when she was young and could have a real love, just not with him?

Juliet wrote to Paul to say she was getting thrown by the fluctuating tone of his emails. We were not his priests. We were his daughters and we needed his protection. This was his chance to protect us and to right the past. We were not the source of his relationship trouble though we had been blamed for it. While it was about love for us, she feared it was about power for Paul.

Paul did not respond to Juliet.

In the unlit garage, when Paul was leaving for good, Juliet begged Paul not to go. She told Paul that he was being an idiot. He needed to get real. Juliet told Paul that if he left, he would never come back, but he would always want to, and he would place the burden of his yearning on us.

Paul called me. He was in his car, he had me on speaker. His voice was rough, he was still surfacing from this respiratory thing. Eva's wedding was in ten days. He had just spoken with Judd. He had called Judd because he needed a friend. Sigrid was angry with him. She had been so patient and then her patience had run dry. She told Paul *the thing about indecision is that it stalls everyone around you.* She was finished with being the other woman. She had a life to live, dreams to dream, men to fuck. Would Paul be one of them? She had closed the door on Paul. Now when Paul called, Sigrid wouldn't answer. He admitted that he could have been more generous with Sigrid. Over the course of those three days, he had been pretty cold. He had underestimated her. Paul judged Sigrid to be an incomplete person because she was so visibly completed by Paul. Paul mistook love for insufficiency. I heard the drone of his sunroof opening, the flare of a match being struck, Paul was smoking. He said he had been driving aimlessly until he saw that he was in no state to drive. When he pulled over, he found himself on Sigrid's street. He was parked under the only tree in her neighbourhood. Her neighbourhood was built from concrete. Outside, children set off fireworks. Women swept and set tables. Men barbecued shirtless. Paul sat low in his driver's seat. He felt like a creep, he said. He did not want Sigrid to see him, but he did need to see her.

Paul told me that when he called Judd, Judd had offered him their spare room. What was Paul to do? Return to his marital home and set up camp in the spare room while Judd climbed into bed with Natasha? It was like some kind of cosmic joke.

Idling outside Sigrid's apartment, with me on the other end of the line, Paul conceded he had been greedy to ask that I give Natasha his manuscripts. Paul said he felt like an addict but could not even name his addiction. How does a man get better when he cannot identify his disease? It was as if every Fellini movie were playing at once inside him. Life was rushing at him, Paul said. Time had no order. A sharp intake of breath. My God. There she is. There is Sigrid. She was locking her front door, holding her laptop bag. She wore a shirt covered in flowers. There was no wind. Only the sun on Sigrid. She was boarding her bus. She did not look like a woman in love, but like a woman who had come through love and her ordeal was now Paul's alone to bear. Paul was speaking to me, but in the echo chamber of his car, he was also speaking to himself, to a novel in progress. He was practicing feeling. After a pause, Paul said that he respected the candour of my refusal. What refusal? I asked, thinking when had I ever refused Paul. Paul recounted the afternoon I had visited him at the storage locker, the afternoon I found out I was pregnant, I had pulled the shopping bag from my wrist and left Paul with his pages. I told Paul what Natasha had told me. She was doing her own thing these days. Paul said he wanted nothing more than to make the same claim for himself.

I felt my mother's presence in the apartment. I felt Juliet's. Some hours, I felt Paul's. His calls and texts came less frequently, I knew he was calibrating. Pregnancy was a bordered space; I felt the borders of myself. I shut myself in and willed time to pass. I left only for appointments with midwives and doctors. I sat in those sanitized rooms, listening for the manic knock of the baby's heartbeat. I watched as Wes tried for a straight face while recording with his phone the sound waves of our child's heart. On the ultrasound screen, Wes and I stared at the ghostly figure, the astronaut floating grey-blue and pixelated, joined to me by a cord. *Stay*, I told our child. Outside, it sunned. Outside, it hailed. I kept still and I wrote. All around me, there was activity. Ani reupholstered the couch. She sewed curtains and hung them in the front window, making a show of opening and closing the lengths of velvet, adjusting the light levels, blowing out the room then shrinking it to nothing. Wes replaced the ancient kitchen counter, the bathroom mirror. He plastered and painted over the water stain in the corner of our bedroom ceiling. With the furniture piled, Wes waxed the living room floor then laid down a new rug. When he repositioned everything, he perfected the angles as if following tape marks on the ground. I felt like we were putting on a play. We were building a set, preparing for a life. Wes spoke with the landlord, gave him high-proof alcohol. The loose wires in the foyer were cleaned up and covered. You would never know that shining, tangled brain lived just above our entryway. Wes went to his studio. I knew he was building a crib. He would bring the crib home only when it was time. Incrementally, I had guarded faith that time would come.

. . .

Paul called Cherry to tell her that Judd had offered him their spare room and he was deliberating it. Cherry told Paul to stop licking his wounds and come home.

Tell me, Paul wrote to me and Juliet from his study, what do I have to my name? He had done the last of the cigar ads. He had done the last of the Scotch ads. He was no longer the face for anything. His bank account was dismal. He could not even buy a coffin. Paul had to admit that being back in the big house, he felt comfort again.

Eva's wedding was in a week.

Paul wanted to be a good man.

Cherry said the only stress in their relationship was his daughters. Aside from your daughters, Cherry said to Paul, our relationship is as good as any relationship can be.

Paul heeded Cherry's comments. In them, he felt his own erasure, but also that he was not to blame.

—

Cherry spoke sotto voce. *Bad things happen when you are with your daughters. You just need to tell your daughters that I will be with you wherever you go.* Sometimes, when Cherry spoke in this quiet, swallowing way, Paul did not know whether Cherry was being serious or playing a game. Regardless, he found the work of guessing galvanized him. Paul felt relief inside himself as, with Cherry, it was clear who he needed to be.

Always look forward, Paul wrote to me and Juliet, never look back.

.   .   .

Eva woke up wanting nothing to do with other people. It was the dawn of her wedding day. The sun had just started to rise. It crept over the horizon and began to spread its whiskey-orange glow. Through her window, Eva thought the sun looked tacky, like something you would spray-paint onto the side of a van. In the corner of Eva's sleeping cabin was her wedding dress. It hung sealed in its body bag, long, white, slender, a simple construction. Cherry called it minimalist, and that was what it was. Cut on the bias. Little room for error. Cherry had collaged wedding photos of John F. Kennedy Jr.'s wife, the one who had died alongside him in that plane crash, Kennedy had been flying the plane. Eva did not know why tragedy behaved the way it did, parcelling itself out so unfairly, destroying some people while leaving others completely untouched. Tragedy shouldn't favour the way it does. Eva heard her stomach growl. She was hungry. In her mind, she travelled to the main house. She pictured the stocked fridge and the full, tidy cupboards. She would go into the kitchen. She would look at all the food. She would not put any into her body. Eva grabbed a sweater from the peg and pulled it over her nightgown. Stiffly, she made her way across the rocks toward the main house. Her fiancé had stayed on the mainland with her brothers last night. Who knows. Maybe he loved a stripper now. Maybe she would never see him again. Maybe he would stand her up at the altar, and she would have to find someone else. Maybe a person could never fully be trusted. Eva entered the main house. It was a glass square. In it, she felt like a specimen. The lighthouse swept its beam over and over the still-dark room as if interrogating it, cutting it to pieces. Eva let herself be inside then outside of the light. She taunted the light. She had gone from asleep to awake. There were no mid-states for Eva. She flicked on the coffee maker. A man sat up on the couch. Eva startled until she remembered the man was her father, the man on the couch was Paul. He ran his hand through his thick white hair. He turned toward Eva, he coughed and then, groggily, asked her how she was feeling. Eva did not answer him. She did not acknowledge his presence. She acted as if he were not there. Tonight, in front of her guests, in front of her parents-in-law, she would be his daughter, but until then, she was angry. She was angry at Paul and her anger organized her. Without her anger, she would flail. Paul had sent Eva an email ten days ago. Tentatively, she opened it, expecting Paul to disown her, to tell her he had never truly loved her, he had only loved Mona and Juliet. The body of the email was the speech Paul planned on making tonight, in her honour, as father of the bride. It was full of ravishing praise. It was not so overblown that it came through as fake, like hagiography. Paul delved into Eva's accomplishments in a concrete way, he made sweet jokes at her expense. He wrote as if he knew her and adored her. The speech had undone Eva, but then she composed herself, and thought, Words are only part of the equation, actions are the other and they hold a far greater weight. Eva was testing Paul's actions.

Paul came to stand beside his daughter at the coffee maker. He smelled of wine from the night before. Eva's stomach rotated. In the corner of her eye, Eva could see her father's face was bloated, his lips were stained an oxblood red from the wine, he looked feral as if he had slept outside. He looked like a castaway. Eva edged away from her father. Excuse me, Paul said, and he reached for a coffee cup. Eva ignored him. Leaving the glass square, she took her coffee back to her sleeping cabin.

When she entered the cabin, Eva's dress was floating like a spectre. There would be no one to zip her into it. No one to place the crown of flowers on her head. Cherry would do both of these things, Eva knew, Cherry would busy herself like an insect around Eva, but in the best stories, it was always the bride's sisters who readied the bride.

Eva would feel there were too many photographs of her and Cherry together.

Eva looked out her window. She drank her coffee. The sun was up now, an understated disc in a weak blue sky. Beneath it, the party tent. The party tent had been set up the day before, and its roof and sides bulged then caved with the gusts of wind coming from the north. The sight of the party tent unsettled Eva. To Eva, it looked like a living thing inhaling then exhaling, standing there empty and worn out, but gloating, like the wedding had already happened, and Eva had missed it. She was an unmarried woman alone in a cabin. A strong wind shook the pane of glass, and Eva thought forward to her swim. There would be extra resistance today. Had she trained as hard as she could? She pictured her arms like axes chopping through the black water, the propulsion of her legs, fighting and kicking, she would compete against the water, she would compete against all of nature. Eva wondered if Cherry was awake yet. She looked over at her mother's sleeping cabin. Mornings were hard for Cherry. Mornings were confrontational. Eva knew her mother stayed in bed long after she'd woken up. Yesterday,

Eva had slid the door open to Cherry's cabin in a panic. Her mother had been lying there, too still. Oh, look, the barge. The barge was crawling toward the island. Eva felt she saw some menace in its shape, it advanced slowly like a tank. Near it, the water crashed against the shoals, looking sharp and white as teeth. Piled high on the barge were the stacks of collapsible tables and chairs. The linens, the wine glasses, the silver. Eva knew the flowers would be on the barge. Her heart ticked like a bomb in her chest. She wanted to see her crown. Eva walked swiftly down to the dock to meet the barge, feeling Antoine following her and then alongside her on the uneven path, getting in her way. Antoine tried for Eva's attention, brushing against her legs, looking up, bounding beside her, but then he gave up, ran ahead, and barked at the strange metal mass coming toward him.

It had been annoying for Eva to see those photos of Mona on the internet. After Wes's big fight with the director, the internet excavated all the old production photos of *Hamlet*. There was Wes, the tormented Prince, and there was Mona, his tragic Ophelia in her floral crown. Eva knew her wedding guests would have seen the photos too. When Eva walked the flat rock that evening toward her fiancé, and said her vows, the guests would see Eva in her floral crown, but they would see Mona more. Eva paced the dock. Her eyes scoured the barge. The arrangements should be there, the crown should be there, but all she saw were wilted heads, a mess of dead flowers.

.   .   .

Lee did not take her own life. But, two years after Paul's affair with Sigrid came to its end, Lee contacted Paul. Doctors had gone in to operate on a perforated ulcer in Lee, and found that she was full of cancer. Lee had six weeks to live. She wanted Paul to know. With Cherry, Paul made an excuse to explain why he was leaving the house that evening. Paul drove across the city. He entered the familiar, nondescript apartment building, square and beige, cut and built like the rest, but inside it, Paul thought to himself, inside it. And he took the elevator and went to Lee's deathbed. He knelt there and he told Lee that he loved her and he would always love her, and that they would meet again in the next life.

When it was time, Paul spoke these same words to Natasha.

He would die before Sigrid.

He would die before Cherry.

At Paul's funeral, only one of his daughters would be permitted to speak.

Eva.

FIVE

The server I recognize from before is standing there at the door to Paul's favourite restaurant. He is older now, the corners of his eyes and his jaw are softer, his clothes are looser, his body is disintegrating downward, back to the ground. Looking at the stroller, he says, Congratulations. And then he gazes up at me and tells me my baby is very beautiful. He asks if I need help. No, I'm fine. I thank him, and pull the stroller up the single stair, edging it through the front door of the restaurant. The server motions to the rear corner. Paul sits at his usual table with his back to me, he is studying the menu. For a moment, I watch my father. This is the day Paul will meet my daughter. River is five months, it is September, but the air still feels like summer, it sweeps through the restaurant's open door in warm, rolling gusts. Outside, the sky is a moody grey, clouds rest full and low to the ground, the late-afternoon light is fading. I wheel the stroller through the mostly empty restaurant. A woman sits alone by a window. The woman smiles at me. She sees a mother in a white dress with her new child.

There she is, Paul says in his amiable way. He stands to greet me as if no time has passed. I push the foot brake on the stroller, and Paul pulls me into him, holds me to him, the hard barrel of his rib cage, he holds me so long I feel the divot in his chest. The heave of his breath, and Paul releases me. Thank you for agreeing to see me, Paul says. He peers down into the stroller. River is sound asleep, she slept for the duration of the walk to the restaurant. I fold open her blanket a bit, she hardly stirs, her arms are above her head like she has just dropped from the grey light. Paul jokes, She looks just like me. I have to pee, I tell Paul, and I ask him to watch her. I'll be right back. Don't wake her, I say. Deal, Paul says. He stares at the baby. He stares into the baby and searches for the lost parts of himself.

I walk back through the restaurant in my dress, it is the only dress that fits my body right now, it has buttons down the front for when I need to feed the baby, it is sized for a much more voluptuous woman, I fill the dress. I descend the tiled stairs. I do not know what to do with my hands, my hands are never empty. In the stairwell, I brush by a sous chef, and I feel sexual, like a panther, I look at him, we look at each other, and then I slink by him, low-bodied and aggressive. I feel his eyes on my back, under my dress. I reach the washroom on the dim, lower level of the restaurant. I enter the washroom, lock the stall door, and listen for River.

In a few years, I will watch River burn with a fever. Oh God, Mama, she will say, I'm seeing everything twice, and then she will smile up at me, momentarily returned to herself, and then she will say, I feel active, I feel like I want to scream, I'm trying not to scream, Mama. She will get croup, and

between her ragged coughs, she will wheeze, and turn to me
wild-eyed, searching for her breath, I am the source of her
breath. I will lay her down on the bathroom floor and run
the shower. I will close the door and window, fill the bathroom with steam, knowing this can't do much, but the
helpline said try it, or take her outside into the cold air, so
I will do this too, I will hold her in my arms in front of our
apartment building, River and me wrapped inside our blanket, no separation between us, a single entity watching the
night. River's eardrum will burst. She will have sensitive
skin. She will trip and break her left wrist. She will fall off
the end of the public dock and into the cold lake, and I will
follow her in and lift her up over my head into the lowered
arms of a stranger. Close call. I will look at my daughter, I
will look at my daughter. This dreamy girl, hair kinked like
a veil over her shoulders, standing before me in the school-
yard, and she will say, Mama, did you know that the French
word for bread is *pain*? All the time, Wes is there, but I notice
him second. It took sixteen hours for River to be born. She
was born blue. She did not make a sound when she was born,
and she was rushed away from my body, and placed on a high
metal table under a bright white light. The midwives ignored
me, they ignored my one question. They patted River's feet,
they patted her face and her chest. The midwives said, Come
on, Come on, Come on, while I could only see a boy there, a
lifeless boy again. Is he alright? Is he alright? Is he alright? Is

he alright? I kept asking the midwives. And then the baby let out a cry, and the midwives put the baby on my chest. Eventually, they said, It's a girl, by the way.

My daughter looked up at me as if to say, What now?

No one warned me that with your child comes death. Death circles your growing body, and once your child has left it, death circles her too. This is why mothers don't sleep. This is why mothers don't look away from their children. This is why, even with a broken heart, a mother will bring herself back to life.

I wash my hands. I gaze intently at myself in the bathroom mirror. I am no longer the daughter meeting her father, auditioning for his love. I am the mother. I am love.

My breasts tingle and spike and shoot hot milk. I adjust the pads in my bra. I smooth my hands over my dress, over my competent body. I have not slept for months. The seasons hardly matter. I've never left River with anyone other than Wes. I push open the bathroom door. I can hear myself panting. My feet slide in my sandals. I climb the empty tile stairs back up to the daylight.

Paul feels they are running out of time. Time is closing in. His body hurts. When his body hurts, a storm is coming.

Mona is so resolute in herself, it is beautiful to see her this way. Toward the end of her time at theatre school, he'd had dinner with Mona. It was early spring. She was in rehearsals for *Hamlet*. It was easy between them. He could see she was in love, but she would not talk to Paul about it, only to say it was impossible, they could never be together. I'm like you, Mona had said, I love what I am not supposed to. I love what I can't. We're the same, Mona had said. The young man she loved had told her that day she should be the one playing Hamlet, not him. Anyway, Mona had said to Paul at the dinner, hold on to this for me, and she pushed a photo of herself across the table. It was a passport photo, black and white. I have one copy, you take the other, she'd said. She'd had the photo taken earlier that day right after the young man had made his comment to her in the cafeteria. She'd left the school, walked to a corner store in the cold and had the photo taken. She wanted to see what he had seen. Love is reinvention, Mona had said to Paul that night. They were drunk when she said it, and Paul had wanted to say, You reinvent me, when I see you, I feel reinvented, but it sounded trite to his ear, and besides, the comment was misdirected, Mona had been speaking about a love interest. But Paul knew what she meant.

Dad? Mona is back at the table, looking between Paul and the baby. She peeks into the stroller. The baby is fine, a blush in her cheeks.

What is it? What's happened? What's wrong?

I don't know, Paul says, and he laughs to himself. I have this new habit. I just start weeping. Don't look so concerned. It's always a momentary thing.

And his daughter sits down. She reaches across the table and she holds his hand. She just leaves her hand there in his, and she studies his wide blue veins.

What was so urgent, anyway? she asks. Why did you want to get together? Oh no. Are you sick? Is that it?

I needed to see you, Mona. That's all.

Paul has ordered a bottle of red wine for us. The wine is poured, we release our hands, we touch our glasses and drink. He looks well. He looks older. I do too. He wears an expensive looking T-shirt, his skin is tanned. Paul tells me he spent most of his summer up north on the island with Cherry. Cherry is keeping bees now, did I tell you that? Paul asks. No, I answer. I am still looking for the perfect shelter, Paul says. The perfect shelter is a woman's body, Paul says, and he laughs. Paul likes being hidden away for the summer. He misses his friends, but he misses strangers more. He likes himself better with strangers. He misses what strangers bring out in him. When people know you well, you perform within the confines of their view of you. With strangers, you encounter new parts of yourself, you're more alive, Paul says, and I watch his mouth move, I see the scrape of his razor all around his mouth. I tell Paul I understand. When I acted,

I felt what strangers brought out in me. I tell Paul that making an entrance from the side stage is like climbing onto the back of an animal many times your size.

I don't know how you did that, Paul says. That took guts.

I guess, I say. But it's also playing someone instead of being someone.

Paul tells me the *Daughter* project in Japan has stalled, postponed a year probably, adding, Only the Japanese could turn a nearly two-decades-old novel into a theme park. And then Paul says, You know *Daughter* was based on you.

I'm sure you've told the same thing to Juliet.

We laugh.

You had to have known it was you, Paul goes on. The father asks too much of her. He leans on her too hard. She gives him support without pause, when he hardly deserves it.

Paul apologizes to me from behind a fictional father.

I look down at River. She is still asleep, she has been asleep for two hours, a good long nap, my breasts are swollen with milk. I pretend to stroke River's face, but hold my hand just above her mouth so I can feel the heat of her breath.

Paul asks me how the new play is coming along. I tell him it's not a play. It's a novel. A novel, Paul says. Yes, I answer. What happened to theatre? Paul asks. Nothing happened to theatre. Theatre is immortal. I'm the thing that changed. I tell Paul I finished the manuscript just before River was born. I wrote like my hands were on fire, I say to Paul, laughing. I knew it would be my last chance for a while.

Terrific, Paul says. Wow, Paul says, terrific.

And I was on bedrest, so.

Paul skips over this. He tells me it was a mistake for Judd to publish his books as a trilogy, to release them all at once. He forgives Judd. Judd no longer understands the marketplace. Paul doesn't either. And anyway, the marketplace is not why I write. Paul leans back and pours more wine, he drinks. The marketplace is the last organism I want to understand, Paul says. Now I have to decide how to live the rest of my life. Maybe I'll self-publish. I'll self-publish for the readers who matter to me. You, Juliet, Natasha, Judd. Art should be separate from commerce. Anyway. I'm only saying this because I didn't make any money.

I dip my French fries in mayonnaise and look around the restaurant. It is as if the houselights have come up. There is grime in the corners, a coating of dust on the plants, I see for the first time that the plants are fake. Paul asks me what my book is about.

I can't tell you exactly, I say to Paul, but I can tell you that I couldn't practice fiction the way I did before. I couldn't dramatize. Why do all that inventing when life gives so much and takes so much away?

Paul nods and drains his glass.

What will you call it? Paul asks, his voice always so low. When I was a girl, his voice was a net and it held me.

I look away from Paul. I watch River's chest rise and fall.

A NOTE ABOUT THE AUTHOR

Claudia Dey's most recent novel, *Heartbreaker*, was a Northern Lit and Trillium Book Award finalist. It was named a best book of the year by multiple publications and is being adapted for television. Her plays have been produced internationally and nominated for the Governor General's, Dora Mavor Moore, and Trillium Book Awards. Dey has worked as a film actress, a guest artist at the National Theatre School, and an adjunct professor at the University of Toronto. Her fiction, interviews, and essays have appeared in *The Paris Review* ("Mothers as Makers of Death"), *McSweeney's*, *Literary Hub*, *Hazlitt*, and *The Believer*.